DAL SEGNO

By

A. Isobel Sutcliffe

JaCol Publishing Inc.

ISBN: 978-1-946675-11-8

For information regarding permission, write to:

JaCol Publishing Inc.

195 Murica Aisle

Irvine, CA 92614

818-510-2898

Editor-in-Chief: Randall Andrews

Managing Editor: Jessica Collins

www.jacolpublishing.com

Acknowledgment

Dedicated to Herb, Tristan, and Maxine for suffering my obsession. To Randall Andrews, my editor and writing coach, for your expertise, patience, and inspiration. Karen Brosinsky Edwards for the cover art and Maggie McGarvey and Jessica Collins for the format editing. D P Lyle, MD for helping me to get away with murder. The legendary E Greg Valencia for proofreading my Spanish.

Table of Contents

The golden light of redemption

shall shine upon you.

1

2014.

Light humidity caressed Raffi's skin as he savoured the sea-salt air of Sydney. An afternoon storm filled the air with petrichor and eucalyptus. He shortened his strides to that of an old man he followed through the jet bridge. Raffi's eyes closed as he breathed his homeland's longed-for and happy scent; tension eased from his body as his feet found Australian soil after too long away.

"Welcome home, Mr Cheney." The immigration officer stamped his passport.

"Thanks." Raffi turned before the man might recognise him. Head down, he made his way to the taxi stand, the backpack on his shoulder his only luggage.

The name Rafael Cheney had held the Australian public riveted for a few months; he hoped they'd forgotten the headlines two years before. The Sydney Airport was pristine compared to where he'd spent the intervening years. El Rodeo, a stinking, dangerous, and overcrowded prison fifty kilometres from Caracas in Venezuela. As he waited for a taxi, his mind wandered to the morning they had set him free, four weeks before.

"*Número Nueve ocho cero, Cheney!*"

Raffi had shouldered his filthy rucksack and picked his way through the sweaty bodies of his fellow prisoners, his heart rate elevated—he'd believe it when it happened. He stopped in front of the two *guardiáns* and gazed down at the man who had called his name and number.

"Cheney," he had said.

"*Firma aqui.*"

The man had held out a clipboard and a pen. Raffi, his Spanish quite good after two and a half years in Venezuela, had signed the form. The man tore off the top copy and gave it to him with his passport and documents.

"*Espera allí.*" He pointed at a group of a dozen others and Raffi knew what to do.

"*Gracias.*" He had taken his place in the line-up and resisted a jubilant dance. He'd walk free, three years early.

He didn't know why they released him, certainly not for good behaviour. Good behaviour wasn't possible in that hell-hole. Perhaps they had needed space after yet another crime wave. Whatever the reason, two years in a Venezuelan prison had taught the twenty-four year old to keep his nose clean in the future. He'd deserved the drug charges; he'd needed the money and it proved easy. A few trips from Venezuela to Columbia and Guyana; he'd made a killing. Then Felipé, the junkie son of the Colombian drug lord, Manuel Carrel, had tried to rob him. Raffi had smacked him around a bit, but young Carrel was still a walking, talking, zombie-junkie when Raffi left Bogota and made his way back to Caracas. The *Policía* had dragged him out of an inner city bar with accusations of murder; they threw him in the *calabozos* where he had huddled for two weeks amongst the sweat and filth of thirty others. When his father arrive with a lawyer, Raffi's gratitude spilled down his cheeks, but they couldn't keep him out of prison—drug trafficking, guilty—murder, not guilty. They sentenced him to five years in El Rodeo. He had survived because he'd traded with a fellow prisoner whose time was up—his best pair of Levi's for a gun and a box of bullets.

"Promise me you'll only use it in self-defence," the older man had said. "In here you learn to duck or you learn to nod, but hopefully with that hogleg, you won't have to get into the habit of doing either."

Many in El Rodeo owned guns and they used them. Raffi had used his on two occasions. He never wanted to think of those times again.

"De esta manera!"

Raffi fell in line as they ambled towards the gates. Some of those released mingled outside as though they didn't know what to do once free. Raffi knew what not to do. He would not take the prison bus, Manuel Carrel's people were bound to stop and search it, he'd be foolish if he thought the drug-lord wouldn't know of his release. He hiked the back roads and footpaths, back to the edge of Caracas and arrived exhausted at Luciana's *chabola* on the edge of the *barrio* just before dawn.

The flimsy back door pushed open with ease. He shook Luciana but she didn't stir. She lay dead still, he checked; she had a pulse.

Not dead, stoned.

He pulled open the pantry door and dropped to his knees.

Yes! Proceed with plan A!

The money he had hidden remained, along with the filth and cockroaches. Luciana was a good root but a poor housekeeper and Raffi thanked her sloppiness. For two years, she hadn't known about the fifty seven thousand US dollars in his money belt, taped underneath the bottom shelf of her pantry. He decided not to wake her; better she didn't know of his brief visit. He removed his shirt, strapped on the money belt and re-dressed; as he opened the front door, he missed a weight on his shoulder.

Fuck! My backpack! As he turned back, a man moved nearby and the suppressed spit of a silenced gun cracked the darkness. Something stung his cheek and smacked into the wall.

"Shit!" Raffi dived back into Luciana's kitchen, snatched up his backpack, drew and cocked his gun. The silhouette of a man appeared in the door, his outstretched arms aimed a gun around the room, searching for his quarry. Raffi fired from three paces and the man dropped his gun and fell kicking to the floor. As Raffi fled, he kept his gun ready; he didn't know if he had killed the man and didn't wait to find out. His survival instinct had lent him speed as he tore away towards the middle of Caracas. As he ran, he checked behind, dogged by the backstreet terrors of this third-world city. He should have known Carrel would have an assassin waiting for him at Luciana's place. Raffi's face burned and bled where the bullet had skimmed his cheek.

As if I don't have enough scars already.

He didn't hire a car, Carrel's people would have such places under surveillance, and for the same reason, he dare not fly to the USA, the airport would be crawling with Carrel's men—all airports of Venezuela. He had to assume the drug lord would have anticipated Raffi's every move. When he had reached an industrial estate five kilometres from the city centre, he made his way to a small motors workshop. He paid an inflated price of fifty US dollars for a second-hand motorcycle and a full-face helmet and set off for Calabozo. He had taken the longer route; the less time spent travelling through Colombia the safer he'd be. He travelled the sultry back roads and had stopped only for fuel and food. When exhaustion overwhelmed he moved well off the road and slept on the ground, gun in hand, with only his jacket for warmth and his backpack for a pillow. He steeled himself as bugs crawled over him. Exhaustion couldn't stop him jolting awake; El Rodeo had left him with many terrors. The frequent sound of wild animals sniffing around woke him but none approached.

He had eluded Carrel's men during that journey and torturous weeks later he arrived exhausted in El Coca, Ecuador. He checked into a hotel, showered and slept for twelve hours. The next day, he bought a new backpack, new clothes, a haircut and a shave; all he needed to face civilisation again. He boarded a plane for Lima. From Lima, he flew to Auckland, and home to Sydney.

****

Happiness spread across Raffi's face as the taxi stopped in front of his mother's house. Antoinette Cheney had lived there since before Raffi's birth. A beautiful house in a leafy suburb, his father's gift to his mistress. The carefully tended front yard had changed little in six years. A wheezing and scuffling made Raffi recoil, an old dog galumphed at him from beside the house. Two years in prison left him with hair-trigger reflexes. He puffed a sigh of relief.

"Is that you, Sid? Sid, good boy! Come here!"

This elderly fat Labrador had barely grown into his feet the last time Raffi had seen him, but the dog's nose remembered his scent. Raffi laughed as the tail-wagging mutt showered him with love and slobber.

The front door opened and Raffi straightened. Two little boys stared at him with anxious eyes.

"Who are you?" The bigger boy pushed his little brother behind him.

"I'm your big brother, Raffi. You must be Nicholas and he'll be Patrick."

The boy nodded, his eyes widened. "Mum!"

"What is it Nic?"

"It's Raffi!"

A cry of disbelief came from inside and Raffi saw his mother for the first time in six years.

"Raffi!" she laughed and cried. "Oh god, it's really you!"

She squeezed the breath from him. Nic and Patrick stared; his little brothers wouldn't remember him. Patrick wasn't born and Nic just three years old when Raffi boarded a plane for the USA, a month before his eighteenth birthday. The gap year before university had turned into six.

Six years that could well be sixty.

He'd long discarded his ambitions of a university degree.

Raffi had asked his parents to stay away from El Rodeo; he hadn't wanted them to see him in such a place. They'd had to make do with letters and photographs.

His mother's arms around him brought warmth back to a frozen heart. On his first night in El Rodeo, already hardened to the wild side of South America, he wasn't ashamed at the memory of tears as he lay on the stinking prison bed and worried about her. She had changed little, her face bore the strain of Raffi's misadventure but at forty-one years old, Antoinette Cheney was still beautiful. Small and a little plump.

Pregnant to a then thirty five-year-old married man, she'd born her first son just before her seventeenth birthday. The scandalized whispers hadn't stopped until Raffi's little brother, Nicholas arrived when Raffi was fifteen. His father hit fifty-nine and still married to a woman around sixty-seven.

That's if the old dragon is still alive.

Raffi followed his mother into the house.

And her continuing existence would be all the proof I'd need to confirm my atheism.

"You should have called to let me know you were coming home."

"Mum, I was too busy getting out of Venezuela, I didn't have time to buy a phone or even find a phone box." Raffi noticed his little brothers staring. "Come here, Nic—Patrick." He held out his arms and nine-year-old Nic moved hesitantly into Raffi's embrace. He could see himself in his little brothers; both had the same black eyes and curly dark hair. "I'm sorry I took so long to come home, Mum."

Five-year-old Patrick chewed on his thumb knuckle, feet planted wide and he swung his body side to side, his eyes fixed on Raffi, not ready to trust this stranger who said he was his brother.

"Oh Raffi, it's wonderful to have my three boys together. Promise me you'll never go away again."

Antoinette sniffed and her dark eyes glittered. "When they sent you to that prison, I thought I'd never see you again."

"I didn't think you would either, to be honest."

"You look so thin!"

"I always was skinny, Mum."

"You need my cooking to fatten you up."

Nic inhaled, his eyes widened, and he snatched up his mother's phone.

"I'm going to call Dad, Mum."

"Does your father know you're home?"

Raffi shook his head and smiled. "Like I said, I was too busy getting home to tell anyone I was coming."

Thirty minutes later, he greeted Pat Rooney, his father whom he'd last seen two years before. It pleased Raffi to see him kiss his mother on the lips as he came in. Why he hadn't divorced the dragon-lady and married her, Raffi could never understand. He guessed it had to do with Pat's wife being a vindictive old bitch who would take him to the cleaners—big time, if he divorced her.

"Why didn't you tell me you were out of that stink-hole, boy?"

"I'm glad to see you too, Dad." Raffi smiled at his father.

His father, several inches shorter than Raffi, was superficially tough and gruff but inside dwelled a soft heart. His eyes sparkled as his son released him from a bear hug.

"I would have told you Dad, but I was busy riding across South America trying to get to Lima. I had a rough ride for a few weeks, but I saw the sights too. South America is a beautiful place."

"Tell me you're done with seeing the world, son."

Raffi laughed. "There's a lot of it I haven't seen yet."

"Antoinette, talk to your son!"

"It's okay, Dad. I've learned my lesson, now I'm going to find a job and settle down for a few years."

Inspiration stole across his father's face. "I might just have a job for you, boy."

"Doing what?"

"Picking fly-shit out of the pepper for your uncle."

Raffi laughed. "I can do that."

"No, seriously—I have a job for you."

2

1988.

Sunday afternoon, the corridors empty, the house staff had finished and gone home. Shirley Delaney pushed the cleaner's trolley to room 705, the one room the house staff never cleaned; 705 was Shirley's job. That day marked the end of an era, the following day the new owner would take the keys to The Wakeley Arms Hotel and Shirley would lose her manager's position.

She stripped the sheets from the bed, picked the towels up and set about cleaning the room. As she dusted, she pulled the video camera out of the flower arrangement in the corner, unplugged it, and rolled the cord.

My little money-spinner. She'd miss the income that camera had provided over the past five years. Her girls kept eighty percent of what the johns paid; for her twenty percent, Shirley gave them a safe place and protection from the police. At 41, she still did a few johns herself but they mostly wanted mothering—tell her their troubles. Some wanted to abuse, some wanted abuse. A clergyman regularly paid her double to whip his hairy arse before she gave him the works.

Whatever floats your boat, Honey.

She earned big money, blackmailing the wealthy clients—deliver a copy of the video with a letter; an envelope of cash in exchange for her silence—they invariably paid up. She'd netted a few big ones, among them the Archdeacon and a federal government senator. They had paid handsomely.

As the cloth zoomed over the full-length mirror, she paused to admire her reflection. The tummy tuck had worked a treat. She drew back her shoulders and tweaked her new hairdo.

"Looking good, Shirl." No longer a nubile twenty-year-old, she had taken care of herself. She had two sons and the eldest, Oliver, had gotten out of control since her husband passed on. Oliver was born before she married

Owen Delaney, 27 years her senior—tall, dark-haired and handsome. He fathered Dylan, the younger of her sons.

Back in her office, she looked at the letter from her employer that she must reapply for her job when the new owner, Mr Patrick Rooney took over. She knew of Pat Rooney, former NRL star, who didn't? She collected her bag and keys and left the office. A good night's sleep would set her up for meeting in person, the man who, if all went according to plan, would be her next husband. Most of Shirley's plans fell together like a Chinese jigsaw puzzle—what didn't fall into place could be coerced.

Shirley had grown up in Newcastle; her mother a hooker and her father unknown. They had lived in a fleapit in the poorest part of town. Her mother put her to work at fourteen and Shirley quickly learned her best assets, pretty face, long legs and big tits. As a pretty 22 year-old she'd had no problem stealing 49 year-old Owen Delaney from his wife. Shirley lived for the conquest, and if that conquest included breaking the heart of a wife or girlfriend, so much the better—*maximum gratification.*

****

"Sorry, Shirley but I intend to manage the place myself. The job of housekeeper is yours though if you want it."

Shirley turned from the whir and chatter of the dot matrix printer and smiled. She didn't need to feign interest in Pat Rooney, an exceptional man—handsome and wealthy. Already, she had checked out the length of his thumbs.

"Housekeeper sounds wonderful—managing this place has often been difficult having two boys to care for on my own."

"Two boys? Where is their father?"

Shirley staged a perfect smile fade; she feared the sparkle of tears might be a little excessive. "He passed on a few years ago."

"I'm sorry to hear that—come to me if you need to organise your time to suit your home life."

"Thank you. It wasn't so bad while my mother was around but—" Shirley turned back to the printer.

"You've lost your mother too?"

Shirley nodded and tore the blue and white printout along the perforated line. "Well, I'll just take this to maintenance." A tremble in her voice and a tilt of her chin. "Can I get you a coffee on my way back?"

"Yes, thank you. Strong white, one sugar."

Shirley let her eyes linger on Pat's for a moment then slide down to his open collar. She left him with a wistful smile and a lingering hint of Chanel number five. *So far—so good, Shirl.*

Shirley became the writer, stage manager and director of her own charade. The first act roused his chivalry, the second—his admiration and trust then his lust. She created a dispute among the house staff to make them all look petty—each cleaner had their allotted level to tend but when Shirley swapped carefully cared for equipment between floors and overstocked two linen cupboards to the detriment of others the proverbial shit hit the fan. Shirley emerged smelling like a rose and resembling a first rate diplomat. She made sure Pat overheard her dress down the maintenance staff for lax effort; she'd spent a week spraying a mixture of hydrogen-peroxide, vinegar and salt into the door hinges in the hotel rooms. It didn't take long for guests to begin complaining about squeaky doors. In various rooms she had sabotaged the toilet cisterns to make them trickle all night; the receptionists compiled a list of complaints from irritated customers. Rice dropped in the restaurant after the cleaners had gone home, a smear of grease on the kitchen wall—everyone but Shirley needed to lift their game. When all ran smoothly again, Pat congratulated her on her organizational skills. When she lured him to her place for a night of expert (but not too expert) sex the Chinese jigsaw was almost complete—any pieces that didn't fit could be hidden under a rug of bonhomie. A piece threatened to pop out when she stirred up her fourteen-year-old son, Ollie, with a view to show Pat how difficult a life she endured with two unruly sons. She over-did the provocation and her son grabbed her by the throat. Pat arrived on the scene in time to see her trying to placate the fractious teen. He calmed the boy and comforted Shirley.

Getting her hooks into Pat Rooney proved easier than expected; he didn't have a wife or girlfriend to hinder her. The first single man with whom Shirley had had a relationship, and when he proposed she feigned reticence—waited a full thirty minutes then said yes. She insisted on a quiet wedding with only a Justice of the Peace to witness.

Pat thought she was publicity shy—Shirley knew of the big mouths and their knowledge of her past.

3

1989.

Pat swayed to rest against Shirley's office door, his weight sent it crashing back against the wall. He pushed himself upright and arranged his face into a rum-soured snarl.

"Why didn't you tell me you're a fucking hooker?"

"You wouldn't have married me if I did."

"You bet your arse I wouldn't have."

"And my boys needed a father—"

"Your boys need a mother, that's what!" Pat teetered on his heel, stumbled down the corridor to his office, and slammed the door.

It had to be some kind of record; his month-old marriage was cactus. When he met her she seemed good natured—not the sharpest tool in the shed, but she had loved him and he loved her—or so he had thought. Three days into his honeymoon, Pat noticed a change in Shirley—a niggle here, a nag there. Moody as a brown snake in the springtime. When she lifted an arse-cheek to let one rip at the breakfast table, Pat's *manoir d'amour* developed dry rot in the basement.

"Even the foulest fullbacks have better manners than you, Shirley." Pat walked his cup to the sink; he didn't think he'd drink tea again.

"I am what I am, Pat. The same girl you married."

"Girl, you say—"

She'd been a whore in the bedroom and a lady in the dining room when he'd begun dating her, now she was a whore everywhere except the bedroom. A couple of days after they'd returned from their honey moon, the truth fell upon Pat like a ton of bricks. Pat found Joey Streeter and Freddy Stevens perched at The Sportsman's Bar, sipping beer and watching the TV on the wall.

"Joey! Just the man I want to see."

"G'day Pat, what can I do for ya?"

"I need a little fixit job on the van, can I bring it around tomorrow?"

"Righto Pat, what needs fixing?"

"I need a new shock absorber put in."

Freddy had piped up and Pat learned what he should have seen months ago.

"I dunno about a shock absorber, Pat, but you got a cock absorber sitting at the end of the bar there. Old Shirl's absorbed more cocks than I've had hot dinners."

Joey snorted into the froth on his beer.

Fucking hell, Pat! How does a man in his mid-thirties get so easily duped? How could you not recognise a hooker?

Now he'd discovered her true profession, he couldn't bring himself to go there.

Like pissing in a public toilet—it's convenient but your own is better.

Pat could get plenty of women on the side but he'd had hopes for his marriage. Those hopes faded in keeping with Shirley's hair colour.

4

Pat hung up the phone and stared at the figures on the note pad in front of him. He should be dancing a jig around the room but somehow he'd lost his enthusiasm for making money. A cool three million dollars sat in his personal bank account, not a bad profit.

"Not bad at all, Pat."

During a slump in the economy, he had bought an old pub for half a million, spent two million fixing it up and now he'd sold it for five million.

This is what it's all about, Pat—shame you don't have someone to celebrate it with.

His marriage was doomed, yet he'd been too busy to kill it off.

His office was on the ground floor of the Wakeley Arms Hotel-Motel. Ten floors high, much larger and newer than the one he'd just sold, Busy improving the Wakeley, he would put it on the market in a few years. Then he'd look at buying into the nightclub market, his dream since his teens.

He sighed, picked up the phone again and poked the kitchen's number.

"Yeah Frankie—send me in a sandwich and a coffee, please? Cheers."

The receiver clattered back into its cradle and Pat grimaced. He swivelled his chair and put his feet on the corner of the desk, laced his fingers across his stomach and closed his eyes.

A soft knock on the door and his lunch had arrived.

"Come in!" Pat's impatience gave a growl to his voice.

Why the sudden onset of good manners?

Frankie—Francois Cheney (arrogant frog-fucker) never bothered to knock; he would have barged in with Pat's lunch, stuck it under his nose and dashed back to the kitchen. The apprentice chef was a right little tear-arse.

The door cracked open then swung wider, Pat's feet slipped off the edge of the desk and he half fell out of his chair. As he scrambled back into his seat, a girl entered with his lunch and Pat fell in love with a brain-lurching crash. As she set the tray down their eyes met and her cheeks turned pink. Pat thought his own cheeks might have turned some obscene shade of purple. His power of speech faltered before he mustered a "Well hello! Why haven't I seen you before?"

She smiled and her steady gaze held his.

"I only started today—"

"What's your name?"

"I'm Antoinette—Frankie's sister."

"Frankie?" Pat's synapses had redirected his intellect through his gonads to have the sharp edges blunted. It took a moment to remember Frankie. He clamped his jaw shut. Antoinette was small, slim but not skinny—just enough curves to make Pat's breath catch in his chest. Her raven hair pulled back in a loose chignon; she had her brother's black eyes, but hers were softer. Her skin a clear alabaster; her lips full and shining pink. Pat wanted—needed to kiss them. "Ah, yeah—Frankie. He said his sister…"

Why didn't the little fucker say his sister was a baby goddess?

"Will that be all, Mr Rooney?"

"Who's—ah yeah. C—Call me Pat."

She turned back as she reached the door and smiled again.

"Don't forget to come back for the tray." Pat tried to keep the plea from his voice. He began to regain control of his faculties, but lose charge of his body.

Please come back for the tray—I'm missing you already.

When she closed the door, Pat made an "aw" noise and rose to adjust his junk; the boner needed more room.

Pat ate one sandwich and drank half the coffee. He would have her; he had to have her, but she looked too young. He rose and went to the main office, found the girl's tax declaration and groaned. Just sixteen. Age of consent. Probably not age of propriety. Pat's veins burned, his nerve ends tingled; the erection subsided but had not disappeared.

Just stand by, old boy, stand by.

When he got back to his office, she had collected the tray. Pat pouted his disappointment and found an excuse to visit the kitchen. She had signed off and gone home. He checked the roster; she was on the lunch shift every day except Friday.

The next day, Frankie barged in with his lunch, Pat gazed past him out the open door and resisted asking him where his little sister was—he wanted to look at Antoinette, not her scrawny brother. She would be busy serving counter-lunches.

Pat decided to take a walk into The Park Lane Bar, talk to the clientele, perve at the new waitress, serve a few drinks and perve some more at the new waitress.

When she noticed him enter the room she smiled and blushed, Pat sent her a look of pure lust; he couldn't stop himself. Little Antoinette made Pat's bells ring a golden symphony. If he never had another woman, he had to have her. As he made his way along the corridor to his office, she emerged from the kitchen and Pat chose the saddest pickup line ever uttered by a besotted human male.

"Little Antoinette, where have you been all my life?"

She turned bright pink and smiled up at him.

I know where you've been, cutting your baby teeth, learning to walk, learning to talk—growing into the most beautiful girl I've met.

The days crawled by and Pat's obsession grew. On her days off Pat grew restless and irritable; distracted on the days she worked. Each morning he invented an excuse to go to the kitchen until—

"Make yourself useful or make yourself scarce!" Frankie brandished a soapy frying pan. Pat ignored the apprentice's cheek and hung about chatting to the attractive waitress—after all, he owned the kitchen.

Antoinette came into his office to collect his lunch tray and gave him her lovely smile, soft lips pulled back over her perfect Miss America overbite. If he didn't kiss those lips today he'd waste away to a shadow by morning. His breath quickened as he beckoned and rose; she timidly approached. Pat cupped her face in his hands, leaned down and covered her mouth with his, softly until her arms went around his neck, pulling him closer. Pat drifted out of reality as his tongue explored her mouth; he hugged her to him. He shivered at the swell of her pert, round breasts against his chest. As he lifted her skirt, a noise somewhere along the corridor startled them apart.

Antoinette snatched up the tray. "I should go—"

"You should stay, honey—I'm just getting started."

Her black eyes sparkled and her breath came in dainty puffs.

"Your wife—"

"Don't spoil this—"

"But don't you love her?"

Pat shook his head. "Nuh."

Not the way I love you sweet girl.

He took the tray, set it on his desk and stepped over to lock the door.

"Now where were we?"

"Pat—"

"Hey, I'm not going to rape you. Not unless you want me to. I'd rather seduce you slowly—like this." He kissed her again; his fingers stroked her smooth neck, then her shoulders, soft and warm, down her arms to hold her hands. "We can take it slow."

"Pat, I've never—I don't know—"

Pat smiled, "I'll teach you."

"My friends all say it hurts the first time."

Antoinette was a strange combination of woman and child. She looked him in the eyes as she spoke. She allowed him to hold her against the length of his body with no reticence but here she confessed her inexperience.

"It doesn't have to hurt."

"Will you be my first, Pat?"

"I'll be your first and your last—whatever you want. Your only would be wonderful. But not here. Somewhere away from this place."

****

Grennie pretended to clean the broom cupboard in the first floor staff corridor. Antoinette had gone into Rooney's office and had remained in there for fifteen minutes. He wanted a piece of that shapely French arse and hung about hoping to catch her on her way back to the kitchen; he intended to ask her out. After ten minutes, he began to fret; he fumbled and dropped a mop bucket on the hard floor. At fifteen minutes, he began to sweat.

She's too fucking young for you, Rooney.

Grennie, the roustabout, earned a good wage, drove a nice V8 Commodore—though beside Rooney's Mercedes, it looked piss-poor. Grennie loved to brag he was good mates with Pat Rooney, ex-NRL star and all-round tough guy—handsome—he didn't even have a broken nose like many footy stars. He had loads of money—everything Grennie aspired to.

You cunt! Now you're gunna take my girl and all.

His lip curled as he watched her emerge from Rooney's office, blushing, smiling, and looking ruffled.

I'll take the leap out of your gallop, Rooney. I'll tell your missus.

****

Shirley was in a pissy mood and the appearance of the roustabout in her doorway flared her nostrils.

"What!"

Grennie stood before her, looking sly.

"Um—Shirley, can I have a word?"

"Go on."

"I don't want to cause trouble…"

"Spit it out, Grennie and stop wasting my time."

"I really don't know how to tell you this, Shirley—"

"Just lay it on me, boy."

Shirley's brow crinkled as Grennie sidled up with his bombshell. "I think Pat is having an affair with the new waitress."

Shirley blenched but a thick layer of foundation and blusher hid it well. She didn't think Grennie noticed.

"He is, is he?" Shirley had only seen the new waitress once when she passed her in the corridor near the kitchen—Shirley's bitterness had spilled from every pore.

Too young and too pretty.

"I'm sure of it."

"Okay, get back to work and keep your mouth shut."

It didn't take long for Shirley to confirm Grennie's newsflash and for the first time in her life, she faced the pain of betrayal. Defiant, she decided she didn't care, as long as he never asked for a divorce. When he'd stumbled on the truth, Pat decamped. Before his spot in her bed had grown cold, a new man had taken his place but Shirley still enjoyed the reflected glory of Pat's fame and money.

Screw him—self-righteous prick, everyone knows about footballers and their gangbangs.

****

Friday afternoon, Pat booked a room at a hotel in a distant suburb. He left Antoinette waiting by the lift as he picked up the key. For a moment, he questioned his motives but her smile quashed his doubts. She slipped her arm around his waist as he unlocked the door to number 505, the honeymoon suite.

"It's not too late to change your mind, Antoinette." Pat led her into the bedroom.

"I'm not going to change my mind."

"You won't regret it."

Neither of us will regret it, I hope.

He pulled the bed covers back and advanced on her. Button by button, kiss by kiss, they peeled off each other's clothes. Pat shivered as she touched his chest and moved closer. Her smooth body against his gave warmth like no woman had before. She laughed as he lifted her off her feet and laid her on the bed. He kissed her from her lips down her neck onto her shoulders. He stopped at her breasts, round and firm, her nipples grew rosy and hard as he teased them. He moved across her soft belly.

"Pat! What are you doing?" Antoinette rose on her elbows, surprised as he lowered his head between her thighs. She giggled and writhed as he open her like a flower, perfect and new. She sighed as his tongue slipped skilfully into the soft folds, knowing he was her first man made him harder than he thought possible.

"I'm teaching you how good it feels to be a woman."

"But—"

"Hey, relax!"

Her back arched and she breathed in rapid gasps; Pat positioned himself over her and penetrated her softness. She kissed his neck and she clung tight to him with her arms and legs.

"Is that hurting?"

"A little—but don't stop!"

That's how it started. Every day—somewhere somehow—Pat made love to Antoinette, the love of his life.

5

Frankie watched Grennie slither into the kitchen with eyes flicking this way and that. On the bench sat an array of desserts, Frankie's morning task; he hoped Grennie might attempt to help himself and earn a crack across the knuckles with a ladle. *Go on—try it, Dweeb.*

"Old Pat's looking pretty pleased with himself, ay?"

"Why?" Frankie monitored his desserts with narrowed eyes.

"Getting his leg over, ay?"

"So? Most of us blokes do from time to time—most of us."

Frankie's sarcasm sailed over Grennie's head with three feet to spare.

"So? You should be more concerned seeing it's your sister he's fucking."

Frankie's hand shot out and grabbed Grennie's neck. "What did you say?"

"I said—" Grennie coughed. "I said, he's fucking your sister—he's got her in his office right now—"

Frankie spun the roustabout, swung his boot and kicked Grennie's arse into the corridor. "Get out of my fucking sight!"

Grennie scurried away and Frankie marched to Pat's office. His crashing entry startled Antoinette to her feet but not so quick, Frankie didn't see she'd been side-saddle on the boss's lap buried to her ears in his face.

"Frankie, calm down!" Antoinette patted her skirt.

"You get back to the kitchen!" Frankie directed her to the door.

"I've signed off, remember?"

Frankie turned as Pat gained his feet.

"You dirty bastard!" His open hand connected with Pat's ear and Frankie found himself viewing the carpet at close range, his hand caressing the sweat between his shoulder blades.

"Try that again and next time I'll break your skinny arm."

"Are you screwing my sister?" His demand muffled against the carpet.

"That's none of your business, Frankie." Antoinette's shoes posed before him.

"You're sixteen!"

"And that's old enough—and it's none of your business."

"Frankie, I'm going to let you up but if you try and hit me again I'll bust your chops—big time."

Frankie regained his feet and stabbed a finger against Pat's chest. "I don't fucking like this—not one little bit!"

"Nobody's asking you to like it." Pat Rooney's eyes held a warning Frankie couldn't miss—as pissed off as he was.

****

The unthinkable usually happens to those who don't and when it happened to Pat he admitted he had it coming. He'd pushed aside the guilt and misgivings, swept along with Antoinette and consumed by new love's fire. When at last they surfaced to life's cool reality, Antoinette announced the unthinkable.

She cuddled into Pats side. The past twenty-four hours had tortured and tested him more than the victorious 1986 NRL Grand Final had. On that night, he ended his career with a hard won victory—the resultant aches and pains still plagued him. Facing Antoinette's parents daunted him more than the toughest opposing team ever had but he had managed to win their trust. Now Frankie waved a meat cleaver at him, his face a shade darker than the strip of rib fillet he'd been about to slice.

"You bastard! First I find my sister in your lap with your tongue in her mouth—now she's up the duff!"

"Calm down, Frankie!"

Frankie ignored his sister and lunged for Pat's throat. "You cunt! I'll have your miserable balls—"

"It's all sorted—I've talked—"

"Yeah—what? You gonna get it aborted? That'd be fucking right—"

"I'm having the baby, Frankie." Antoinette's hand pressed her brother's chest.

Pat loved Antoinette for her calm demeanour; it soothed the testosterone crackling in the air. He buried the notion of pulling the cleaver from Frankie's grasp and inserting it in his bony arse.

"I'm buying Antoinette a house. I'll take care of her, don't worry."

"You fucking better or I'll slice your dick off!"

Fucking chefs and their obsession with knives— slicing and dicing.

"If you don't quit waving that thing at me, Frankie, I'll flush your head in the toilet! Now get back to work!"

"Um—right." Frankie jiggled the cleaver and turned back to the steaks.

6

1992.

The last light faded from the sliver of clear horizon as the youth set off into the dusk. Tonight he would lose his shackles and become Blitz; tonight he'd launch a crusade of fear. His discarded birth name lay behind with society's norms—a mask he'd re-don come morning. Tonight he'd release the pressure—the internal countdown ticked with each step.

Intermittent flashes heralded a storm. Along the darkened beach he strolled past a couple hand in hand— not the desired target. He sought a lone woman, wandering in the night—prostitutes all of them. His hatred masqueraded as a balm for the hurt inflicted by the women who should have nurtured him, but in truth, it fanned the flame of resentment. Blitz played to his ordinariness—ambling along the beach, head down, hands in pockets and murder brewing in his heart. Few people bothered to look—average height, average everything—that night he'd show them how average he was not. He carried no weapon. Darkness, surprise, and lethal intent were Blitz's chosen weapons—and whatever came to hand; the earth would provide. Fat raindrops hurtled into the sand, Blitz greeted them like an ally. He changed course and crunched through the shell grit and pebbles of the high-tide mark, up the splintered wooden stairs to a beachfront park.

He halted as a flash of lightning silhouetted a girl huddled under a gazebo to wait out the storm. Blitz smiled his secret smile. The picket from the rotting hardwood fence came away easily. Blood pounded in his ears, savagery burned his guts. The storm's deluge veiled the scene. As his hand closed over her mouth, the girl panicked, her fight lent strength to his purpose. Down on the concrete floor he tackled her, the cotton dress ripped. Her face shattered under his fist—her body hot and alive with fear. The screams he clamped inside her mouth. He forced her legs apart—push—thrust and again. Force his seed into her. Push and withdraw. His power fed off her fragility. Her whimpers and sobs increased as he zipped his jeans. The picket rough in his grip; she rose to her knees and he swung and hit her neck, a nail bit and tore the soft flesh as he drew back. Her blood spattered his jeans and joggers. Another swing hit her head. Another and another. She landed facedown and arterial blood pumped onto the concrete in a steady, dying rhythm.

Blitz's heart soared as his feet kissed the sidewalk; he sped through the pouring rain. The unleashed monster returned to its lair.

****

The rain had slowed and the streetlights cast a dim glow over the park. The old man ambled across and prodded the darkness with the beam of his torch. The only sound the patter of rain on the muddy ground.

"Hello?" He swore he'd heard a woman scream seconds after the rain had begun to hammer his corrugated iron roof. He had stared into the street from his window, eyes wide. Each flash of lightning revealed nothing.

"Is there anyone here?" He picked his way around the shrubs. Something white near the picnic tables drew his gaze. He hurried through the puddles and stumbled to a halt. "Hello?" His torch light gave up the horror in the dark.

****

"I wish I could tell you more, officer, but the rain was so heavy, I wasn't sure what I heard was a woman scream. I watched out the window but could see nothing."

"Okay, thanks for your assistance. Get yourself home now and we'll have someone come and get a statement from you shortly."

Detective Sargent Will Fishman watched the old man shuffle across the street to his house. Red and blue lights flashed and illuminated the neighbourhood. A growing contingent of uniformed officers questioned curious onlookers. Cars patrolled the suburb in search of the offender.

****

1994.

Blitz sat among the sand and rocks and watched the party from a distance. Teenagers laughed and danced around a beach fire. A youth played guitar and sang while his friends clapped and joined him in the chorus. Blitz was about to give up and search elsewhere for his next victim when a girl wandered from the group, she called over her shoulder to her friend who waved a hand and turned her attention back to the singer.

Blitz's eyes narrowed as the girl lifted her dress and crouched close by; he could hear her pee.

Filthy prostitute.

This would be a challenge with her friends seventy metres away, but risk enhanced the thrill. He got to his feet, his cock stiffened; the firelight swayed with the teens. He wrestled the girl into the shadows and silenced her with a punch to the jaw. Her bikini bottom tore easily and he fell upon her. He penetrated her, his hips danced to the music—harder and harder. She reanimated and he clamped her mouth shut, his teeth sank into her soft neck as his orgasm shook him. As he regained his feet, his hand closed over a rock, big enough to heft over his head…

****

Will sat head bowed. The forensic report before him confirmed what he suspected. The serial killer had struck again, the girl last night, Zoe Johnson, from the beach party his third victim. Tahnee Shultz just over a year ago, then a month ago, Karlie McCann. All raped and bludgeoned to death. Outside the press waited to hear more bad news. In spite of the police's best efforts, they moved no closer to an arrest.

Will feared he and his colleagues danced to the killers tune.

Too smart or just lucky, either way…

They had his DNA and fingerprints but still had no leads.

What kind of warped and perverted mind must he have?

An irritated colleague stopped at Will's desk and dropped a folded newspaper before him.

"Fucking journalists! They're feeding this guy's fantasy, I just know it…"

THE SAND DUNE KILLER STRIKES AGAIN. LAST NIGHT ANOTHER YOUNG WOMAN LOST HER LIFE…'

"…Sand Dune Killer—they're giving him super-villain status."

****

"They made an arrest?"

"Yep. We think we've got him."

"Take me to him."

And turn off the recording equipment for just three minutes while I rip him a new one.

Will eyed the suspect through the glass with mounting frustration. Rocky Gleeson's face was white as he whispered to the duty solicitor. No sooner had Will entered the room and the solicitor asked him to leave.

"I need further discussion with my client."

Come on mate—we'll soon know if you're our man so let's get on with it.

Will had applied to have Rocky held until the preliminary results arrived. They had found his fingerprints on the girl's clutch purse. The duty solicitor came to the door and nodded for Will to enter.

The young man perched on the edge of his chair, jiggled his knee and hugged himself.

"Now, Rocky. Tell us where you were between eleven p.m. and midnight last night?"

"I was with my girlfriend, Bessie."

"Bessie Marks?"

"Yes."

"Can you tell me what happened?"

"We—we had a stupid fight!" Rocky's face contorted, his eyes glistened and chin quivered.

"And then what happened?" Will knotted his forearms across his midriff.

This is the big scary Sand Dune Killer?

"She walked off, s—said she was going home."

"What time was that?"

"About eleven, I think. We weren't going to stay late, we wanted to catch the bus."

"And did you follow her?"

"No. I sat there for a minute and then I walked up to the esplanade—I looked around for her but she'd gone. I thought she must have walked up the road and caught bus back into the city."

"What did you do then?"

"I walked over to Deeping Street to the bus stop and I went home."

"Witnesses say they saw a man of your description running fast along the esplanade at around midnight."

Rocky shook his head. "I was almost home by then—I was on the bus."

"The man had a tattoo on his hand like yours; witnesses describe his clothing to match yours. How do you explain that?"

"I can't explain it—please! You have to believe me! Bessie is my girlfriend—we love each other—we—I would never hurt her!" Rocky buried his face in his hands, his shoulders convulsed. Suddenly he looked up. "Why don't you check with the bus driver?"

"We have. He can't confirm it either way."

****

Two weeks passed and Will perused the DNA results. He swore aloud.

"It's not him, Will." Saul, the forensic officer, took a long pull from his black coffee. "There were two sets of DNA inside Bessie, one matches Rocky's and the other matches the Sand Dune Killer—it matches the DNA found in the previous three girls."

"So Rocky is innocent?"

"Yep. Poor bastard."

7

1994.

Dusk in the seaside village of Bundeena south of Sydney.

"How old is she?"

"The victim or her sister?" The young constable eyed the senior officer.

"The victim."

"Thirteen."

"Is she dead?"

May as well be. "No, she's not. She has been raped and bashed."

"Where's the weapon, Constable?"

The young officer pointed to a football-sized rock inside a plastic bag.

"Oh god! You said there was a witness?"

"Don't get excited, she's five years old and she wasn't making much sense."

"Where is she now?"

"Her parents took her with them to the hospital."

"We'll have to try and interview her."

"The victim or the witness?"

"Both."

"I don't like our chances with either, sir."

****

"This has to be my break," Will Fishman set down the phone as his superior hurried in the door. "This one has the Sand Dune Killer written all over it."

"Have they arrested anyone?"

"No, but they have a witness this time and the girl isn't dead, so when she wakes up, hopefully she'll give us something useful." Will got to his feet. "Sarg, let me go over there. I want this bastard so badly I can taste it!"

"Alright, Will. Get your team organised and I'll clear it for you."

An hour later, Will fidgeted in the passenger seat of the unmarked car, wishing the traffic would part and let them through. He arrived just in time to watch the interview; he longed to participate but agreed to observe remotely. The girl sat on her tearful mother's lap and ate jellybeans while a WPC tried to extract useful information.

"Can you tell us what happened to your sister, Lily?"

"Mosie is my big sister." The little girl had a stuffy nose.

"Yes we know, Lily. Can you tell us what happened to her?"

"The man donged her on the head."

"What did the man look like?"

The little girl rocked back and forth. "Ugly."

"Was it one man?"

"He bumped Mosie's head."

"How many men, Lily?"

"He was naughty." The girl's vocal chords drowned in saliva and glucose. She swung her chubby legs, bouncing in her mother's lap.

"Can you tell us what colour hair he had?"

Lily stopped and stared at the WPC. "Nuh." She shrugged.

"Did you see his face?"

"He pulled his pants down."

The mother's eyes squeezed shut, her hand pressed her mouth.

"What colour pants did he have?"

"Blue."

The WPC held up a blue jellybean. "Blue like this?"

The little girl shook her head and shoulders. "Nuh."

The WPC sighed and looked at the detective beside her. "Can you think of anything?"

"He had a picture on his hand." Lily popped another jellybean into her mouth.

"A picture?"

Will shifted to the edge of his seat; his heart quickened at this piece of information.

Lily stuck her finger in her nostril and rotated it. "The man with the rock, he had a picture."

"Can you draw us the picture?"

"Yep."

The detective pushed a note pad and pen across the table and encouraged her with a smile. She hesitated, frowned, picked up the pen and scrawled an S.

"Is that what was on his hand?"

Lily stared at the page and lightly stroked the back of her left hand with the pen. A long moment later, she added two circles inside the curls of the S.

"Are you sure that's how it looked?"

"The other one had a big willy!" Her eyes grew round; a choked sob escaped her mother.

"Was there two men?"

"Yep."

"What did the other man look like?"

"Tall."

"What colour hair did he have, Lily?"

Lily swivelled her shoulders back and forth. "Like that." She pointed at the detective seated opposite.

"Black hair?"

"Yep."

The following morning they brought in a detective trained in child psychology to try again. At his side sat a composite artist with various identikit drawings and a sketchpad. Will watched the little girl, seated on her mother's lap, the end of her pigtail stuck in the corner of her mouth. Her mother dishevelled and devastated; her eyes red and puffy. The detective began on the subject of the family's holiday, gradually working around to the beach outing.

"Now Lily, I want you to close your eyes and try to remember exactly what the man with the picture on his hand looked like."

The little girl's face screwed and she shut her eyes.

"Can you see him, Lily?"

She nodded.

"Can you see his face?"

She nodded.

"Can you see his hand?"

Will wondered if the detective noticed the little girl's lower lip tremble as she raised an imaginary object between her hands.

"Tell me what you can see, Lily."

"His hand—" The girl's mouth squared and she bawled as only a child could, opened her eyes, and the wail modulated up to a piercing scream. Her mother jumped to her feet and clutched her child.

"No more! Please! I can't have both my daughters destroyed." Tears fell into her child's hair. "Please—"

The little girl pressed her face into her mother's shoulder.

"Mummy! Make him stop!"

****

Defeat dragged on Will's shoulders. Somewhere out there a serial killer enjoyed his freedom, stealing oxygen from the world. Did he care about the life he'd stolen from his victim and her family?

The forensic officer laid a folder on Will's desk and placed his cup beside it; the aroma of coffee floated to Will and reminded him he hadn't had lunch.

"What have you got, Saul?"

Their efforts to solve this latest incident had Will frustrated. Apart from having suffered rape, the victim had received a major head trauma, which had resulted in an extensive intracerebral haemorrhage. The doctor doubted the girl would ever speak again and it appeared she was blind. The local police had staged a major operation. They stopped every car on every road out of the seaside town of Bundeena but hadn't found any men with a tattoo on their hand. Lily could do no more than draw the S with two dots; she gave them little else. They circulated her vague description and received a number of reports of men with tattoos on their hands but each of those had a solid alibi. Two of them worked; another drove a truck to Newcastle and the other…

If I don't arrest this bastard, my career will amount to nothing.

Saul took a mouthful and put the cup back on the desk. He opened the file and passed a sheet of paper across the desk.

"We've identified two lots of DNA. This girl was raped by two men and they're related."

"Brothers?"

"Half."

1994.

Pat had locked up after a busy night and set off for the kitchen to see if Ollie, his stepson, had finished the dishes. Pat wanted to get home to Antoinette and their son, Raffi—the sunshine in Pat's life. He would consult a solicitor soon with a view to begin divorce proceedings. Too much time had dragged past; his marriage to Shirley had proved his *error maximus,* the love gone—killed by deceit. Antoinette was his life. He'd tried to set her free, told her to go and live like other twenty-year-olds, unfettered by a man approaching his fortieth year. He had left her with a choice and the following day collected another swat from Frankie. Pat recalled that brief standoff in the kitchen all those nights ago.

"You bastard!" Frankie waved a wooden spoon at his boss, his face dark with anger.

"This is about your sister, isn't it?" Pat rubbed his ear, trying to relieve the ringing and smarting.

"You weak cunt, Pat! She's the mother of your son and you're trying to get rid of her."

Pat ducked as Frankie swung a roundhouse punch; it swished over his head and Pat gripped his arm.

"Frankie! If you hit me again," Pat slammed the tall skinny chef against the cold-room door and made a dent with his head, "I'll drown you in the fucking sink!"

Frankie's left hand clutched the wooden spoon and a handful of Pat's shirtfront. "Why did you break my little sister's heart?"

"Mate, I didn't—did I? I thought I was doing her a favour. I'm too old for her, you've said it yourself."

"Yes, I've said it. But for some strange reason that I cannot fathom, she loves you, you miserable bastard! And you dumped her, just like that!"

Pat stared and a warm honey sensation spread throughout his body.

"You mean—she still wants me?"

"Of course she does, you old dickhead!"

"Mate, you're a good chef, but if you keep forgetting I'm your boss, I might have to find another chef."

"You need my guiding hand, Pat." The wiry muscles of Frankie's forearm bulged as he'd tried and failed to shake Pat.

"Arrogant little frog-fucker!" Pat ceased his grip on the young chef and hurried home to Antoinette. It took a couple of days for the honey to leave Pat's system.

As he entered the kitchen, his attention snapped back to the present at the sight of Ollie backed up to the plate stand, white faced and eyes bulging at something beyond Pat's range.

"What's up, Ol? You look like—"

The back door of the kitchen snapped close, a hiss of a foot sliding on the tiles and a movement in Pat's peripheral vision propelled him to a defensive posture before his stepson.

****

Frankie Cheney had seen off the last of the kitchen staff and flicked off the lights as he emerged from the scullery to put away his tools. He heard voices and suffered a moment's disbelief at the scene before him. Standing in front of the stoves was a man he recognised as Col McInnis; a regular in The Sportsman's bar—a felon, and rumour had it, a hit man. Even in the dark, Frankie could see the gun pointed at Pat who shielded his stepson. Ollie cowered in his shadow, white faced and trembling.

"Hand him over, Pat or I'll put a bullet in your guts!" Col's gun had a hefty silencer.

"I'll do nothing of a sort, Col."

Frankie glanced from one grim face to the other.

"My client wants him dead!"

"You're not going to touch him."

Frankie knew it wouldn't matter if Pat handed Ollie over—the hitman would kill them all, he couldn't leave any witnesses alive.

Dead men tell no lies—or truths.

"Come on, Col," Frankie set his ladles on the bench, "Ollie's just a kid, whatever he's done—"

This guy must be completely stupid to try to take Ollie out in the kitchen. Unless he imagined he could drag him out the back and plug him.

Frankie didn't especially like Ollie, he was a conceited prick, but he didn't think it cause enough to rub him out.

"You're just a kid too! Fuck off!" Col waved the gun at Frankie. "Now Pat, use your brains."

"I won't let you kill him, Col!"

"Then I'm going to have to shoot you both."

Frankie stepped in front of Col and laid a hammer fist over his heart.

"Col! Last warning—stop!"

"Fuck off, kid, this has nothing to do with you!" Col cocked his gun and aimed it at Pat's chest."

****

Pat marvelled at Frankie's nerve, unarmed he stood with his fist against Col McInnis' chest—did he think he could stop this half-mad gangster-come-hitman with just a hammer fist? He watched the young chef pull back his other hand and thump it over the other held against Col's chest.

What are you trying to do Frankie, give him a heart massage?

Col emitted a strangled grunt, his eyes bulged and he wheezed; the gun clattered to the tiles. The hit man slowly sank to the floor and Frankie manoeuvred him onto his back then he dashed into the scullery.

"Frankie? What did you do to him?"

Frankie didn't answer. He hurried back into the room with a wad of paper towel.

Get me that Elastoplast roll, will you?" He knelt, tore open Col's shirt and held the wad of paper towel on his chest. "Hurry up or there'll be blood everywhere."

Bewildered, Pat dashed to the medicine kit on the wall and took out the roll of adhesive plaster.

"What did you do?"

"Shanked him with a steel skewer."

"Fuck! Frankie! He's dead!"

"Better him than you, Pat."

"Ollie, go and get your mother."

Pat watched as the young chef stuck generous lengths of Elastoplast over the paper towel blocking the tiny hole in Col's chest. The only blood to escape he had trapped in the paper towel. He left the skewer in his victim's heart.

"There you go, Pat. Bloodless surgery." Frankie felt for a pulse in Col's leathery neck.

"Jesus H Christ! Remind me never to get on your wrong side, Frankie."

"Pat, I'm gonna go down for this, unless—"

"Not if I can help it, Frankie." Pat stepped forward; Shirley appeared beside him and yelped. "Shirley! Back the van right up to the back door—now." He looked around; "Ollie, go to the laundry and get that dirty-linen trolley—make sure it's empty."

"What did you do to him, Pat?" Shirley leaned over Col.

"Don't ask questions, just do as I say."

With the help of Ollie and Frankie, Pat transferred Col's body into the large canvas bag of a dirty linen trolley and lifted it into the back of the van. He loaded six Besser blocks in behind the trolley and closed the doors. The back of the pub dark, a loan lamp cast shadows of nothing across damp pavement, there was nobody around.

"Okay, none of us is going to say anything, are we?"

"Nobody will miss Col," said Shirley. "What are you going to do with him?"

"I'll work something out. Now Shirley, take Ollie home, and Ollie—I'm not going to ask you why someone took out a hit on you but whatever it is you have been doing, stop it. Next time Frankie and I might not be available to protect you. Frankie just saved your life; repay him by making something of that life. And Shirley, if anyone asks where the linen trolley is tell them I'm getting that loose wheel replaced."

As Shirley's car disappeared in the rain, Pat returned to the kitchen and picked up the phone.

"Sorry to wake you, Barney, how would you like to take a midnight cruise?"

Barney Falconer was a friend of Pat's father, the most loyal and close-mouthed man Pat knew. Pat listened as Barney moaned, yawned and hacked a cough.

"Awright, Pat. Where are we goin'?"

"Meet me at my boat down on the Marina."

Pat hung up. Frankie stood, fists clenched, chest heaving, his eyes on the floor where Col's corpse had lain. His young face drawn and worried.

"What are you going to do with him, Pat?"

"Feed him to the sharks."

"Jesus! Pat—I've really fucked up haven't I?"

"You saved Ollie and me. Thanks Frankie, you're a good bloke. We just need to get old Col onto the boat without raising suspicion; hopefully the linen trolley won't attract the wrong kind of attention."

"I've taken a life—"

"And saved two. Soldiers do it all the time. Come on, let's go."

Pat didn't feel good about it but he would never hand the young chef over to the police. Frankie had saved his and Ollie's life—probably Shirley's too. In the small hours they transferred Col's body onto Pat's motor launch. They removed anything that might identify him and took him for his last cruise, twenty-five nautical miles off the coast; the water roiled and bubbled as he sped to the bottom, tied in the canvas dirty-linen bag, weighted with his gun and six concrete blocks. Five miles back towards the mainland, Pat tossed Col's Rolex overboard. Frankie took a pair of sharp scissors and julienned Col's wallet and driver's licence and dropped the pieces into the Tasman Sea at five-minute intervals. The scissors went overboard after them.

They arrived back at the Marina well after breakfast time.

"Early morning fishing trip?" A man asked as they disembarked.

"Yeah, mate," said Pat.

"Catch anything?"

"Yeah—nah—nothing."

"What kind of bait did you use?"

"The wrong kind." Barney grimaced and spat into the water.

"Worms, mostly," Frankie muttered for Pat's ears only.

****

Frankie Cheney left Australia, he travelled to Europe and the UK; at the year's end, he opted for three months in

Canada. From Canada, he worked his way down the east coast of the USA then around the Texas panhandle to Brazil where he stayed for almost five years. He refined his culinary skills and gained other useful talents along the way. He returned to Australia, harder, wiser and glad to be home.

9

1995.

The birth of a baby is usually a happy event. The pain, the tears, the blood, soon forgotten for joy as that little body, comes into the world. Naked, squalling and kicking. A little creature in the raw form, time and nurture, the perfectors.

In the cold pristine theatre, the midwife's face lacked its customary anticipation—she had no one to encourage, no parent to present the baby to. The surgeon cut into the swollen belly, working through to the uterus. A quick poke and the amniotic membrane ruptured. More cutting and groping—he pulled the tiny head into the world, a wriggle brought the shoulders, torso and legs. Clamp and cut the umbilical cord. The surgeon placed the baby into the waiting hands of the midwife. Delicate cries came from the tiny throat as tender hands swabbed the amniotic fluid, the baby's mouth and nose cleared with a gently applied suction. The surgeon watched as the midwife checked the baby over.

"Apgar is good." She straightened and closed the humidicot and wheeled it away to the Intensive Care Nursery.

The bitter taste in the surgeon's mouth wasn't only the scent of iodine floating in the air. The family and the ethics committee had sanctioned this procedure. Tears welled in his eyes and he silently wished that baby girl the best of life's blessings.

"Go on." He nodded to the anaesthetist.

The machine that beeped life into the young mother fell silent.

10

Pat dropped by Shirley's house to pick up some books, not intending to stay. As he laid them on the backseat of his car he noticed his stepson, Dylan, sitting on a seat in the garden, head down and his hands stuffed in his pockets. Dylan was the younger of Shirley's sons and in Pat's opinion more likeable by far, in fact, Pat would gladly take Dylan off Shirley's hands if the opportunity arose.

"Dylan, what's happening?"

The boy shrugged. At fifteen, he was tall and beginning to fill out, Pat could see he would grow into a handsome man.

"Did you get the part?"

"Yeah—but, I dunno—I think I'll give it a miss."

"Why? You rehearsed for weeks—you were perfect!"

Dylan looked up at Pat and pulled a face. Pat's eyes widened as they took in the boy's black eye and cut lip.

"Shit, Dylan! Have you been fighting?"

"I pissed Ollie off and he belted me."

Pat sat beside his stepson.

"What did you do to piss him off?"

"I was listening to the original soundtrack of West Side Story—you know, trying to get a feel for the songs. He was studying—he came in and did this." He flicked a hand at his face. "He keeps telling me I'm gay. I'm not Pat, I like girls."

"It wouldn't matter if you were gay, Dylan—it's not an excuse to beat someone up." Pat grasped Dylan's shoulder. "Look, why don't I give you some lessons in self-defence. You're nearly as big as Ollie, with a bit of know how you could kick his arse all over town."

"Can you learn that?"

"Bloody oath you can."

He frowned. "I don't like fighting—I don't want to hurt anyone."

"Defending yourself is different to going out and belting someone for no reason." Pat studied Dylan's face; he had a gentle soul. The boy had proved a talented singer and dancer. For the past year, he'd participated in his school's musical theatre productions and spent hours working on an audition for the male lead in West Side Story. Pat worried Dylan would throw away his big chance. "Ollie has been beating you up all your life hasn't he?"

Dylan nodded. "I hate him, Pat. I'm so sick of being punched in the guts."

"Does he do that?"

"He always does it, he doesn't need a reason. He does it when I'm not ready for it."

"Look, come back with me now, to Antoinette's house and we'll get started."

"Can we?" Dylan attempted a smile and winced at the pain of his cut lip. "That'd be great!"

"Go and get your stuff and you can stay the night."

Pat watched Dylan bounce away to collect his things, when he was out of sight Pat followed him into the house and made his way to Ollie's room. He opened the door without knocking.

"Why don't you learn to knock—oh hello, Pat." Ollie clicked off the TV a little late—Pat saw but ignored the porn scene. Ollie rose from his bed. "I was just going to get a drink? Want one?"

Pat pulled his punch a little but it was hard enough to drop Ollie to the floor. His stepson crumpled, hugged his stomach and he turned from red to grey as he struggled to catch his breath.

"I think you know what that was for." Pat muttered. "If I ever hear you've hit your little brother again, I'm coming after you, and I'll break every bone in your miserable body."

Mottle faced, Ollie didn't answer; he groaned and rubbed his middle. Pat grabbed a hank of his hair and jerked his head back.

"Are you listening to me, boy?"

Ollie nodded.

"Good. Don't make me come back, Ollie. The next time I punch you, you'll think you've been kicked by a horse. That's no idle threat."

Pat knew Ollie had a different father to Dylan. He'd certainly lucked out on genetics. His twisted features wouldn't be half so bad if he didn't have that warped personality to match. He attended university, studying political science—learning to make the most of his devious nature. Since the incident with the hit man, Ollie had kept his head down; he didn't often go out except to the pub with fellow politics students. The penchant for beating up his younger brother remained Ollie's last foible and Pat would put a stop to it if he did nothing else for Shirley.

Pat was back in his car when Dylan emerged from the house. He had no idea where Shirley was and he trusted she'd work out for herself where the boy had gone. Dylan often stayed at Antoinette's house, she had become like a big sister to him and he adored his baby stepbrother, Raffi.

11

Pat gazed at Shirley, dozing as Days of Our Lives cast pale blue light on her tonsils. Wet snores gurgled from her gaping mouth. When he'd married her, Shirley was fashionably slim, pretty in an angular way; her short-cropped red hair framed her striking features well, but she'd turned hatchet-faced and rough as a bag of hammers. Her hair had faded to mousey brown; it hung about her collar, dragging on her jaw-line.

Jesus-fucking-Christ, Pat! Why did you go there?

He flopped onto the opposite end of the lounge and Shirley awoke with a snort.

"Pat," she mumbled, "I didn't hear you knock."

"I didn't." *My house—my keys.*

"Shirley, I want a divorce."

"We all want something, Pat." She swiped a drop of drool from the corner of her mouth and rubbed it on her skirt.

"I'm going to see my solicitor tomorrow and we'll begin proceedings."

"The hell we will." She yawned widely and scratched her head.

"Shirley, don't make this difficult."

"I'm not making it difficult, Pat, I'm making it impossible."

"What? Why?"

"You've made a fool of me all over this city and there's little I can do about it. But I can refuse to divorce you."

"I don't need your cooperation, Shirley, I can just."

"You're forgetting something, Pat. I can send you and your smart-arse chef to prison. Then your little French maid will have to cope with the big bad world all by herself."

Pat's eyes narrowed, he didn't miss the implied threat—Shirley had often made threats against Antoinette but had never acted on them.

Frankie worked in Brazil but he'd soon want to return to Sydney. If an arrest warrant waited for him he'd have to go into hiding, never free to return.

"You wouldn't."

"Try me."

"Frankie saved Ollie's life—yours and mine too unless I'm greatly mistaken. I don't know why someone wanted Ollie whacked; I decided I wouldn't ask. But if it wasn't for Frankie, your son would be dead."

"I have it all documented, Pat. You, Barney and that arrogant French bastard you call your friend—I only have to go to the police and you'll all go down. Your little French tart—"

"You won't touch her—" Pat changed tack; better to not aggravate her; malice was Shirley's cake and pie. "Look, Shirley, be reasonable—what we have is not a marriage."

"Maybe not but it suits me down to the ground."

"You can't be serious."

"Try me."

"Why did you marry me, Shirley?"

"I needed a husband—I was a widow, raising my boys alone, they were getting out of control. I needed a man around."

"You didn't need to marry me—you only had to ask for my help."

"My sons needed stability, I did too."

"What you needed was to act more like a mother and less like a—" Again Pat reined in his mouth.

"There's a certain respectability in being married, Pat. But what would you know about that?"

"There's nothing respectable in living a lie. There's nothing respectable in being a bloody parasite."

Pat walked out with the bitter taste of defeat in his mouth.

12

1996.

Grennie Barnes flinched, he'd strolled into Shirley's little office on the second floor, and it appeared empty until the door closed behind him.

"Grennie, I need your assistance."

"Shirley! You frightened shit out of me."

She took a seat behind her desk and propped her elbows on the mess of room reports and linen counts

"I have a job for you."

"Sure—doing what?" Grennie sat, folded his arms, spread his knees and displayed his crotch.

"I need your help to get Marty out of my life."

"Sick of him eh?"

Two months after she'd married Pat Rooney, Marty Downing had attached himself to Shirley like a ravenous shellback; he moved in as soon as Pat moved out. Grennie had thought it generous of Pat to sign the house over to Shirley and keep her employed as the head of housekeeping at the Wakeley Arms Hotel.

"You could say that."

"What's wrong with him?"

"He's as useless as an arsehole on an elbow."

"So what do you want me to do?"

"Help me dispose of him."

"Why can't you just tell him to go?"

"I've tried, he won't."

"And—" *I wonder what Marty knows that he shouldn't?*

"Do I have to spell it out? I want to dispose of him. Whack him."

"That's gonna cost you a pretty penny, Shirl. In advance."

"Five grand cash up front and the same when you've done the job."

"Double it."

"What—do you think I'm made of money?"

"Ah well, can't do it for less." Grennie got to his feet and made for the door.

"Wait—okay—I'll double it."

****

"Fuckin' 'ell, Shirl—yer sure ya got enough Drano or what?" Marty had opened the garden shed looking for a rake, Shirley spent the morning in one of her moods, Marty knew the best way he could keep the peace was do a spot of gardening. Pull a few weeds and rearrange the leaves on the back lawn.

He gazed awestruck.

"I'm storing it, Marty. It's for the hotel."

"Fuckin' 'ay? What, are they shitting turds of clay in the fuckin' drains?"

"Come and have a drink with me, Marty."

"Now you're talkin' my language, Shirl."

****

Shirley looked at the clock; ten minutes to midnight. Grennie would arrive soon. Marty Downing sprawled on the couch. Shirley checked his pulse, there was none—the horse tranquiliser Grennie had procured for her had done its job.

"You had to have last say didn't you, Marty?" As the life left his body, Marty's parting shot was to empty his bladder all over Shirley's favourite couch—around a litre of kidney-filtered rum and Coke. She hadn't thought of that when she had tipped the last of the ketamine down his unconscious throat. "Stupid bastard. Nobody threatens to grass up Shirley Jackson."

Grennie arrived with a tap on the back door.

****

"So, where are you gunna take him?" Grennie eyed the grey face of Marty Downing.

"To the garden shed."

"Shit, Shirl—the neighbours will smell him, won't they?"

"Let me worry about that, let's just get him out there."

"Okay." Grennie hefted the scrawny carcass onto his shoulder. "Lead the way, Shirl."

Shirley led the way through the dark and opened the garden shed.

"Put him in there." She shone her torch into an empty 200-litre plastic chlorine container. It proved difficult, Grennie sweated and grunted as he manoeuvred the body, the container tipped over.

"Hold the fucking drum steady, will ya?" Several attempts later, Marty's corpse slipped inside the drum, his head flopped between his knees and his body released a parting puff of wind.

"Marty's last fart; so what now?" Grennie puffed from his exertion and sniffed his shoulder. "Ah jeez-fuck! He pissed his pants."

"That's all. I'll take care of the rest."

"I'll take the balance of my fee, Shirl." Grennie plucked at his shirt.

"Okay—okay. Come inside and I'll get it for you." Shirley padlocked the shed.

This has to be the easiest twenty grand I'll ever earn.

"So where are the boys tonight?"

"Dylans working and Ollie's out with his uni mates."

13

2000.

"Forget it?"

"Forget it."

Will Fishman glowered at his taciturn superior.

"No! Dammit! It's too soon!"

"Admit it, Will, the trail went cold after the incident at Bundeena."

"But the DNA matches—"

"Matches who?"

"One of those who raped and bashed the girl at Bundeena is our man." Will listened to himself railing pointlessly against the inevitable. "Karlie McCann, Zoe Johnson and Bessie Marks—all raped and murdered in the same way, then there was that girl, Tahnee from Cronulla, the year before—we know it's the same guy!"

"Yes, but you don't know who he is and that is the problem. You have loads of evidence but no culprit, we can't DNA test every male in New South Wales. It's been six years, the trail has gone cold. There hasn't been another since the girl at Bundeena—she died without uttering a word of evidence." Senior Sergeant Dighton got to his feet, strode around the desk, and patted Will's shoulder. "I'm sorry, Will. I know you've invested a lot of time and energy into the case, your efforts have been duly noted—but I can't spare you any more time. There are now more urgent cases requiring your full attention. Write a report and collate the evidence and file it unsolved."

Downcast, Will dragged his feet back to his desk. The Sand Dune Killer had first struck just shy of eight years before. They'd collected plenty of DNA, the guy was blatant. Vicious, but plain lucky. Also fleet of foot; on the one occasion they had found the girl's body within twenty minutes of her death, there was no sign of a suspect. The last case proved the most horrific, the most tragic, and it left Will in spirits so low it hurt.

14

2014.

"Well, here it is Raff." Pat Rooney opened the grubby and squeaking door of Dylan's Blues Club. "Dylan has run it into the ground. Do you really think you can turn it around?"

"I'll give it a red-hot crack, Dad." Raffi look around at the smelly, dilapidated nightclub. "What the fuck? He's stacked beer kegs on the stage? Where does the band set up?" The DJ's booth beside the stage showed signs of human habitation.

"I can't explain what Dylan does. He's too busy drinking and being a dickhead to run this place properly. I'm a bit long in the tooth to run it myself."

A door slammed from beyond the stage and an out of tune singing echoed from the loading dock.

"Oh wo! Come and get it, honey. Oh…"

Raffi watched Pat stride past the stage and slap the singer as he weaved through the door into the main clubroom.

"Where the fuck have you been?"

"Hey Pat! What's doin' old man? *Urp.*" Dylan looked homeless—unshaven, dirty and grey faced.

"Never mind what I'm doing! Where the fuck have you been?"

"On a bender and tied to a bed in a brothel, Pat, playing patty-cake with the pros. You know what those cunts are like…"

Raffi winced as his father swung again. Pat stood shorter than Dylan, but it didn't stop him smacking the big man.

Dylan, a gentle giant was big enough to belt Pat into next week, but his love and respect for his stepfather stayed his hand. He rubbed his face where a welt the shape of Pat's hand had begun to appear.

"What can I say, Pat? I'm a cunt!"

"You're also an unemployed cunt, now go and clean out your office and get the fuck out of my sight!"

"I get the feeling you're pissed off with me—"

"You're sacked. I'm giving management of this club to Raffi."

"Raffi? I thought he'd become a Columbian drug lord."

"He's back and he's going to prove to me he's a better man than you. Now get up there, tidy that fucking office, and get out of my sight. When I want to see you again, I'll give you a call."

"Little Raffi!" Dylan weaved across the room, a cloud of alcohol fumes and brawny arms engulfed Raffi. "I didn't think we'd be seeing you for years."

"You know me, Dylan. I charmed my way out of El Rodeo three years early and here I am, back in Oz."

"You're a fuckin' marvel, Raffi. How did you get out?"

"Got an early release and walked out."

"I can't believe it—I worried you wouldn't get out of there alive."

Raffi lamented. The first night in El Rodeo, he thought he'd only leave the place in a wooden box. "Well here I am, alive and well."

"It's a miracle that drug lord didn't get you, boy."

"I was too clever for Manuel Carrel." Raffi's fingers found the wound on his cheek, a smooth tethering of new skin.

"We'll have a few drinks one night and you can tell me all about it, little brother. We gotta catch up—last time I saw you, you weren't even old enough to drink. Now you're gonna run this gin-joint! Amazing!"

****

From the passenger seat of his father's car, Raffi saw his city through the eyes of a world-weary adult, when he left Australia six years before he was fresh out of high school and heedless of the harsh world he would encounter. His father's BMW cost more than most in South America would see in a lifetime. His city had so much money they could decorate the margins along its arterial roads. It didn't anger him—this country's pioneers had worked hard and suffered much for the lifestyle now enjoyed by its new generations.

"What happened to Dylan? He never used to be that bad."

"Dylan hasn't had the easiest life. He lost his father when he was little and Shirley was never a good mother to him. Now Dylan has split up with Kate—I dunno. I was glad to see him today; he's been missing for two weeks. I worried something had happened to him."

"You didn't sound too glad—"

"I know—it was hit him or hug him—I dunno Raff, I'm not good at emotions. Dylan is every bit my son as you, Nic, and Patrick are. To be honest, I'm not that fond of Ollie, he's the stereotypical politician. Dylan could have had a career in theatre—he was a great singer and dancer. He probably grew too big and tall for dancing—but jeez he could turn it on. He was a legendary barman—the women loved him. He could flip bottles and shakers like an expert juggler, mix it, shake it, pour it and then give the girl a kiss she'd never forget. Tom Cruise and Bryan Brown had nothing on Dylan."

"I'm going to give him a job, Dad. He's going to need it."

"Getting him interested might be a problem. One way or the other he'll have a job, even if it's answering phones in my office. We need to keep him where we can watch him, Shirley doesn't care—as long as he doesn't interrupt her perfect life with his drinking and carousing, she doesn't give a shit."

"Dad, why are you still married to Shirley? Don't you love Mum?"

"I love your mother more than my own life, son. No, Shirley holds the cards that could destroy a few lives. If it was just mine, I take the chance."

Raffi watched his father ease the car through a snarl in the traffic and waited for him to elaborate. As he accelerated away from the bottleneck, his father glanced at him and shook his head.

"No matter— hopefully she'll die soon—she must." Pat Rooney grinned and shrugged. "You don't live to an old age with a nature like hers. Marriage is only a piece of paper, Raffi. In my mind, I've been married to your mother since she first walked into my office. Jeez Raff, you should have seen her—"

Raffi grinned, by the age of four he had begun to appreciate the hold his mother had over his father.

15

Pat had set Raffi to work the day after he returned to Australia, exactly what he needed. By day, he cleaned and laboured for those renovating the nightclub; in between, he sat in his office, making plans and negotiating with debtors over the phone. Each night he dreamed he was still in El Rodeo where men with sharpened iron bars loomed out of the dark. He shot holes in them and they kept coming—he shot and shot until he jolted awake, sweating—the echo of gunshots in his head. He knew he needed to seek counselling but so far hadn't made the call; he feared he might blurt out to a shrink that he had shot a fellow prisoner between the eyes.

That night would stay with him forever.

"Eh! El Canguro!"

Raffi had pulled on his pants; picked up his bag and flung his towel over his shoulder. He turned and reeled back, a hulking Colombian bore down on him with a short, sharpened length of steel rod. The gleaming point nicked his cheek and left a stinging cut. He groped in the side pocket of his backpack and gripped his pistol.

"Fuck off, mate—You've got no reason to have a go at me."

"I have orders from Señor Carrel to take you out, Canguro."

"From the man himself—or one of his lackeys?"

"I kill you, cunt!"

He swung the shank in a downward arc and Raffi was too slow; the steel scraped down his ribcage and made a long, jagged cut. He pulled his gun as the man advanced with weapon raised for the fatal stab to his heart. Raffi aimed, squeezed the trigger and a tiny red hole appeared between the Colombian's eyebrows, the sharpen steel clanked to the cement floor and rolled away. The man crumpled face down and twitching, one elbow poked toward the ceiling as though he might push himself upright.

Raffi wrapped the towel around his ribs and fled. When he stumbled into his cell, Irish Ian lounged on his bunk reading a dog-eared playboy magazine.

"What seems to be troublin' you, young Cheney?"

"Ian, I just shot a dude in the showers!"

"Y' did what?"

"He tried to shank me—I had to shoot or he would have killed me."

"Lie on your bunk—let me see."

Raffi lay down; the wound didn't bleed as much as he'd feared but several exposed rib bones—pink and shiny—made him queasy.

"I can be fixin' it for you young Cheney; just keep the pressure on that gash. I'll fetch some dressings from the kitchen."

Ian, a nurse before he landed in El Rodeo, cleaned and taped the wounds and ordered Raffi to lie still for twenty-four hours. "Unless you need the toilet, I won't be holdin' no potty for you."

Raffi's temperature began to rise within twenty-four hours; he slept fitfully and delirium set in.

"Young Cheney, wake up boy."

"Where am I?" His head and ribs throbbed. "Ian—"

Raffi's skin burned, rivulets of sweat dripped onto the prison bunk, the cell sweltered and concentrated the stench of garbage drifting in the window. Raffi's stomach heaved bile.

"Take it steady, boy. You don't want to be opening that wound again."

"What—"

"I've managed to get some broad spectrum antibiotics for you. Here now, take two for starters."

"Have the guardiáns been asking questions?"

"I told them you skinned your ribs when you slipped on the stairs and the wound got infected. They were happy for me to treat it, they hate having to cart anyone off to the hospital. Besides, the sick-bus is banjaxed."

"What about the dude in the showers?"

"What dude? And which showers would that be?"

Raffi had recovered to his normal, healthy self—albeit sore, scarred and sorry; thankful for the Australian immunisation scheme and the tetanus shot he'd received at the age of fifteen. He'd always be grateful for Irish Ian's effort on his cheek—the scar wasn't bad—in another few years it would be barely visible. The scar on his ribs proved much worse but given the magnitude of the wound, Raffi figured he had plenty to be thankful for. The scar from the bullet crease on his other cheek remained red; he hoped it would fade too.

Overseeing the renovations on the nightclub kept him busy and the tireder he was, the better he slept.

On the first Friday night, he accepted an invite to go to a party thrown by one of his old school friends, who, when he'd discovered Raffi had returned, called asking to catch up. Raffi feared he would have nothing left in common with his old friends but he needed to get his life back on track—get drunk—get laid. He also needed to re-establish contacts, the better his connections, the better his chances of attracting clientele to his club. Pat had stressed Raffi was the one who would make or break the place. If patrons liked the host, if they felt welcome and connected, they'd come again.

The party was at a house rented by a group of friends. Raffi got a drink, propped himself against a wall and watched the small crowd a similar age to himself, some he remembered from school. They laughed and joked and

Raffi forced himself to join in. These people didn't know what he'd suffered in El Rodeo and he wasn't ready to confide. Let them think him the same person that had left Australia six years before.

"Raffi Cheney! It really is you!"

Raffi had noticed a woman watching him and braced himself; he knew at any moment she would approach and sure enough…

"Hello, yes that's me. Do I know you?"

"Raffi! I'm Megan Beltz; don't tell me you've forgotten!"

"Oh Megan, yes. Sorry—it's been a long time." He'd gone out with her a few times in his last year of school. He didn't want to say it but she had gained weight and lost height; he recalled her being taller.

"So where have you been, Raffi?"

"Um—travelling."

Well, at least one person doesn't know you're an ex-con.

"So where did you travel to?"

"The USA and—err—other places."

"For all those years? How did you afford it?"

"I sold drugs."

She laughed raucously. "You always were a funny bugger, Raffi."

Raffi smiled and emptied the dregs into his mouth. "Well, I'm going to get another drink."

He took a drink from the fridge and twisted the cap off. He looked around; Megan talked to a group of women, so Raffi took the opportunity to wander onto the balcony. A tall blonde caught his eye; she stood listening to a conversation though she took no part. He moved into her line of vision and waited. She looked up and her eyes settled on him, he winked and smiled. She sidled away from the group and approached; a little flat-chested and a little fat arsed but after two years of having nothing better to look at than scrawny male, Hispanic bodies, Raffi wanted to feel the softness of a woman.

"You're the dude who went to prison in Mexico, aren't you."

"Maybe."

"What was it like?"

"It wasn't Mexico and it wasn't nice. How about we get out of here."

"Sure, where did you have in mind?"

"Bed. And it'll have to be yours because I'm living at my mum and dad's house for a while."

"You don't mess about, do you?"

"No."

She slipped her arms around his neck. "Dance with me first." She pushed him back into the room where the music blasted from a sound system. She pressed close, and Raffi was glad the room was dark as the boner threatened to burst out of his jeans. He suffered five minutes of dancing before he growled in her ear.

"Come on, girl. Let's go. What's your name?"

"It's Tiffany."

"My name's Raffi."

"I know."

Back at Tiffany's, he removed her dress as soon as she closed the door. She took his hand, led him to her room, and sat him on the bed. Raffi feared he'd cum in his pants as she straddled his lap, their tongues fought for the upper hand as they each delved into the other's mouth. She puffed raggedly as she removed her bra and rose on her knees. The pink tips of her breast soft on his lips and tongue; his long hands cupped them as he teased until she moaned. She clambered to her feet and pulled him upright.

"Quickly, take your clothes off!"

He held his breath as deft hands unfastened his buttons and pushed off his shirt. She removed his jeans, shoved him back on the bed and took him in her mouth.

"Hey, let's cut to the chase—it's been two long years."

She laughed and climbed onto him, warm and tight and Raffi fought for control. He lasted roughly a minute before he cummed hard into her.

He luxuriated in her smooth curves, they talked, made love and talked some more. Around three a.m., Raffi got out of her bed, dressed, and slipped away while she slept.

No breakfast at Tiffany's for me.

16

Mia Colter held her grandmother's cold, thin hands and watched her breath fog the clear mask covering her mouth and nose.

"Oh Mia—" Tears sat in the hollows of her eyes and Julie Colter dragged in oxygen, each lungful distressing and painful. "What's going to become of you?"

"I'll be alright, Nanna, I'm nearly nineteen and I'm taking good care of myself."

Mia did worry though; while she sat there with her grandmother she lost money. On a Thursday night, she earned around twenty dollars an hour busking, but she feared to walk away, she might not see her Nanna alive again. Mia hoped her band would get some work soon; the boys grew restless with rehearsing twice a week and no gigs. They could have had a gig at Dylan's Blues Club, but when Mia went to see the manager, the interview didn't go as she'd hoped.

"Sit down, Mia."

Mia took the chair beside his desk and inched it away for fear the haphazard stack of paperwork might slide into her lap. It approached midday and she could smell the alcohol fumes emanating from him. Dylan Delaney was a big man; well over six feet tall and well built. In his mid-thirties, the skin beneath his indigo eyes puffed as though he hadn't slept and his dark hair needed a comb.

"So," he took a sip from his glass, "You're looking for work?"

"Yes—"

"Do you have any bar experience?"

"No, I have a band and our music is suited to this venue."

"You're a muh—hic—magician?"

"Musician. Yes, I delivered a promo pack last week, your office lady told me to come and see you."

He rubbed his face and muffled a burp. "Ah, did she?"

"You can listen to us on YouTube. We—"

"Take your shirt off and I'll give you a job."

"What?"

Dylan staggered to his feet and hiccoughed.

"You got a lot going for you, pretty girl—"

Mia jumped to her feet and tried to put the chair between them, he smiled and set it aside. His hand closed around her wrist and he pulled her towards him.

"Don't! Please!"

"How old are you, sweetie?"

"Let me go!" Mia swung her boot into his shin."

"Ow! Hey! I get the f—hic—feeling you're not interested?"

"Glad we're on the same page, mate!" She pulled from his grasp and fled.

Mia shuddered as she remembered his hot breath on her neck; he had reeked of rum.

"Mia." Her grandmother held the mask away from her face. "My things, my valuables, they're in storage. The key is there in my purse. Take it Mia."

"But Nanna, you might need it when you get out of here." Anguish thinned Mia's voice.

"I'm not coming out of here, Mia. No! Listen to me, darling, don't cry, please. I won't be around much longer. You must be brave and Mia, you must take care of yourself."

"Nanna…"

"Promise me, Mia, you'll always put your own safety first."

"I promise, Nanna."

"Now, take the key. I want you to have it."

Mia nodded and blinked away the tears; her trembling hands searched in her grandmother's purse and took out the key for a storage shed. Her grandmother was her only remaining relative, her grandfather had died when Mia was two and she had no memory of him. Mia's mother had died within hours of giving birth to her. Her grandmother wouldn't talk about it. The only other relative she'd had known, her aunt Lily, died five years earlier. Mia had only heard Lily speak on three separate occasions, unless you wanted to include the times she screamed in the night. Mia's grandmother said Lily had bad dreams.

At thirteen, when Mia practiced for a piano exam, Lily had come into the room to listen.

"Hi, Lily," Mia said.

Lily smiled vacantly and clapped her hands as the tune ended.

"Would you like me to play some more?"

Lily nodded and clapped artlessly.

Mia begun again and Lily moved closer, she came alive as the melody flowed from under her niece's slender hands. Mia flicked to the next page and played on. Lily watched over Mia's shoulder. Mia mashed the keys as Lily screamed in her ear and ran from the room, down the hall, the house shook as she slammed her bedroom door.

"What happened?" Her grandmother scurried into the room, swabbing her hands on a tea towel.

"I don't know, Nanna. Lily was watching me play and she started screaming."

Three days later, Lily had thrown herself in front of a train.

"Mia, there's one other thing. Please, you must not let Ashleigh abuse you as she does."

"But she's my best friend, Nanna."

"A true friend wouldn't treat you the way she does. Now that you're out of school, try to find some other friends."

"I am, Nanna, I've got my band and they're good friends. Don't worry about me. I know Ashleigh is bitchy but it's just her nature, she can't help it."

"Whether she can help it or not, you don't have to suffer it." Julie Colter pressed the mask to her face and rattled in some oxygen.

"Please, don't worry about me, Nanna. I'm going to be okay, I promise I'll take care of myself."

Ashleigh had become her best friend at the beginning of high school. Mia was a gangly twelve year old; shy and bookish, her peers had laughed at her fascination with Electric and Delta Blues. Ashleigh was a pretty blonde and as they progressed through high school, her popularity grew. Mia often found herself on the outer edge of the in crowd. She refused to dye her hair a different colour, Mia liked it dark brown; Ashleigh declared it boring. Mia continued to grow and by the time they finished school she had grown taller than average and towered over Ashleigh. Her best friend began to find fault with Mia's appearance—

too tall, too thin. If she wore a tight T-shirt, her boobs were too big—in tight jeans, she looked sluttish—in loose pants, she looked sloppy. Mia tried to ignore her friend's catty remarks and bit her tongue when Ashleigh wore skinny jeans that accentuated her short, thick legs and big bottom. When Mia auditioned to join a blues band, Ashleigh predicted she'd fail and when she got the job, Ashleigh accused her of showing off or more likely they only hired her for her looks—not that Ashleigh thought Mia pretty or anything…Mia detested teenage girls and thought by eighteen her friend would have risen above such immaturity.

Her grandmother grew ill in Mia's final year of high school and she took the role of carer. She denied herself the enjoyment of a social life. She had to listen to other girls discussing their boyfriends and the fun they had on the weekend. A boy in her year, Christopher asked her out on many occasions, but Mia only managed a few dates. Between school, busking and rehearsals with her band, Mia had to clean the house, get the groceries, and drive Nanna to the doctors. On the night of her high school graduation, Mia left early; her grandmother had taken a turn for the worse and the doctor sent her to a hospice. With the help of a social worker, Mia had moved out of the rental house and into a share house with two of her band.

Her Nanna was fifty-one and Mia feared the end drew near. Emphysema from years of heavy smoking destroyed Julie Colter's lungs. Throughout her childhood, Mia had never known her grandmother to have close friends; she kept to herself and family. Mia was her last living relative; when asked, Julie would reveal nothing about the family of her birth, other than, "They're all dead."

Three days after her nineteenth birthday, Mia got the call. Her grandmother would not see another day. She arrived at the hospice with just enough time to say good-bye. Nanna passed away leaving Mia alone.

17

Raffi made coffee in his mother's kitchen when the back door opened and closed.

"Frankie! Just the man I want to see!"

Frankie Cheney flinched at Raffi's greeting. Latin America had sharpened his reflexes too.

"Raffi! I heard you were home! It's good to see you, boyo!"

"Yes! Back home ready to make my fortune."

Raffi hugged his uncle and suffered having his hair ruffled.

"Sacré bleu! You have grown tall! You're taller than me now; they must have fed you well in El Rodeo."

"Venezuelan swill three times a day, packed with dodgy goodness. Speaking of swill, I'm going to need a chef; are you available?"

"What do you have in mind?"

"You want a coffee?"

"I'd love one. So, what—"

"A French-Cajun café."

"Sounds interesting. I'd have to quit my job at the Grand."

"There's no hurry, I only put in the plans for approval a couple of days ago." Raffi clipped the filter basket in place and reached for a coffee mug. "Once that goes through I'll have to find the money, but I'd like your help in setting it up if you can spare the time."

"I'll talk it over with Sherrie. I'd be happy working for Pat again." Frankie's wife, Sherrie worked as a bank manager. They had two sons and a daughter. Frankie, a stay-at-home dad until their youngest went to school, had taken a part time job.

"You'll be working for me. Dad owns the place and he's putting up the finance to get the nightclub running again, but I'm the manager. I haven't discussed the café part of it with him yet. I might have to organise my own finance."

Raffi often wondered about his uncle's unswerving loyalty to Pat; they were as close as two men could be. Raffi and Frankie, too, had always been close. Raffi bore a strong likeness to his uncle, tall and wiry—curly dark hair and black eyes.

"So, are you looking for Mum? She'll be home soon, she drove the boys to school."

"No, it's you I came to see, Raffi, I've been hearing a bit of chatter." Frankie leaned against the kitchen bench and appraised his nephew.

"Chatter? What do you mean?"

"From South America."

"Like what?"

"There is talk that you are in danger. Talk that Carrel's main assassin will be out of prison soon."

"I'm back in Australia now, what can he do to me here?"

"He can kill you, Raffi." Frankie lowered his voice. "No don't laugh—you'd be foolish to think he doesn't have connections here. I'm sure he has."

Raffi rubbed his chin and said nothing. Frankie's words reflected those Raffi himself had already considered in quiet moments; he just didn't want to admit it, not even to himself. It would terrify his mother to know danger lurked in her son's background. Raffi had encountered Carrel when he had befriended his son, Felipé.

"Did you manage to get inside Carrel's compound?" Frankie checked the hallway.

"Not right inside—not to where the man himself lives. I could have got in, I know how but without a small army I'd never attempt it."

"You know how to get in?"

"Sure, he has an escape route. His compound is hard against the cliff face of a small mountain so any raid would have to come in the front way and that is heavily fortified. He has an old mine shaft he can use as an emergency exit, it leads right through the mountain and comes out about half way up the other side, it's hidden in thick undergrowth."

"And you know where it is?"

"Sure. Felipé took me into the tunnel. He wanted to take me right through but I squibbed, I didn't think it was a good idea to walk into the nest of a cut-throat drug lord."

"Come, Raffi—see my father's empire from the inside." Felipé pushed through the greenery and beckoned Raffi to follow.

Raffi peered into the darkened tunnel, around him the sounds of birdsong and the beauty of a lonely mountainside. His shirt clung to him in the humid air; it was a long hike from the road up to here along an overgrown path.

"Won't your father object?"

"He's not home, he's in Rio, living the highlife."

"So who is in charge while he's gone?"

"My big brother, Agg."

Raffi shuddered, Agg Carrel was infamous as far north as Chicago. It tempted him to see Carrel's compound from the inside but given what he knew of Agg, he erred on the side of caution.

"What's in there?"

"A luxurious casa. Then there is the lab and a nursery for Papa's crops. A high wall protects us from the Policía. The people of the village love my family. We look after them, and when we need a favour, we choose from *many volunteers. My father is a rich man, which is why I went to school in the USA."*

Raffi took in his friend, Felipé—the red eyes with their pinpoint pupils, the gouge marks on his arms and purple needle scars on his skinny neck. An expensive education hadn't stopped Manuel Carrel's son from becoming a victim of his father's enterprise—impaled on his father's sword.

"Felipé was a bloody dickhead, always stoned off his face—I'm surprised his father has survived so long given how much bragging his son did. About an hour later he tried to rob me, his brother had refused him entry to the lab and he was desperate. I'd just made a delivery and had about sixty thousand US dollars in my pocket—I wasn't going to part with it so I slapped him around a bit. He swore at me in about five different languages and I left. I intended to come home to Sydney soon after. He was dead within three days—his head caved in with an iron bar. I was back in Caracas by then but they still arrested me for it. I really think Manuel's older son might have disposed of Felipé. Now there was a real cut throat—I don't know what his proper name was, everyone called him Agg. I called him Agro, but not to his face."

Frankie's eyes and mouth narrowed.

"So could you draw me a map?"

"Easily, but what can you do about it?"

"I have connections too, Raffi."

Raffi stared. His uncle didn't talk a lot about the time he spent in Brazil. He didn't spend all of those five years working in kitchens; that much Raffi knew.

"Well—go get a piece of paper and draw me that map."

18

Dylan lay back on the bed of his childhood bedroom, swigged scotch straight from the bottle and wallowed in self-pity. He had returned from The Gap where he'd stood gazing at the sea swept rocks far below then turned and hiked all the way to his mother's house. A dull thread of sadness weaved through his existence. It was a good thing, wasn't it, that Pat had given management of the club to Raffi? Like everything else in this life, Dylan had lost interest. He drank himself numb rather than face his demons.

If you had any guts, they'd be scraping it off the rocks, Dylan Delaney. You want to live? Why? Your life has gone to hell; you don't even have a job anymore—or a wife. Seriously, what the fuck? You're living in your mother's house. And who was that girl you fucked last night? She sure was a looker but fucked if you can even remember her name.

Sex was the only thing Dylan took pleasure in anymore—dirty, smutty sex. Everything else—work, family—why bother? Pat, Antoinette, and their kids were his family but they didn't need him. Kate didn't want him. His mother hadn't cared a fig about him for twenty years, she only cared about Ollie. Oliver Jackson, his older half-brother, politician and all round slime ball.

Yeah, fuck both of them.

Dylan looked at the photo of his late father smiling at him from his bedside table—a photo Shirley had placed there a long time ago—most likely when she wanted to appear the grieving widow. He sniffed and mopped his eyes with the back of the hand clutching the bottle then took another swig. He had never known his father—he had only the vaguest memory of him. Pat was the only man Dylan considered his father, without him Dylan hated to think about where he might have ended.

I'm sorry, Pat. I have failed your expectations of me.

There was a knock on the door and Dylan called, "Enter."

Shirley pushed it open and leaned on the door jam.

"Where are your photos, Dylan?"

"What photos?"

"All your photos, family photos—one's you took when you were a teenager."

"Ah—dunno." Dylan took a mouthful of scotch, swallowed and coughed.

"It's important, Dylan. I want to go through your photos."

Dylan squinted at her and smiled. "Getting worried about what might be in there?"

"Frankly, yes."

"Um, I think they're at Kate's place."

"Well, get them."

"Yeah righto."

"Today! Not whenever you feel like it."

"Yeah righto." Dylan took another swig and belched a cloud of alcohol fumes sufficient to propel a small rocket into the stratosphere. A hiss of disgust escaped Shirley; she turned on her heel and stalked away without closing the door.

Yeah, fuck you too, you old trollop.

19

Raffi unlocked the new soundproof doors to the nightclub and pushed one side open. He had just finished showing his father the revamped façade and foyer.

"Well, here it is, Dad." He stepped aside to allow his father into the plush entrance lounge. "I've completely renovated the interior."

He was both proud and apprehensive; being Pat Rooney's biological son didn't give him an advantage over his stepbrothers. His father was a generous but tough man, he expected his sons to work as hard as he did. Pat had forked out a large sum for Raffi to fix the nightclub Dylan had left rundown and in debt. Raffi had spent all of it and more. He'd negotiated with the club's creditors, made a part payment on their accounts, and in exchange for their patience he gave a promise of continuing loyalty.

****

Pat Rooney looked around and nodded; of all the nightclubs he owned, this was his favourite. It could comfortably seat two hundred and fifty people and stand another fifty in the bar. He strolled down the steps into the main clubroom, slid his hand on the polished wooden handrail, and admired the quality. He took in the new dark blue carpet, the plush circular booths along each wall, recessed into mirrored alcoves, and the rows of new tables and chairs along the centre of the room. The midnight blue ceiling twinkled in the dim lighting. Gone, the outdated backlit sign of Dylan's Blues Club, traded for red, white, and blue bent neon tubing that scrawled "Raffi's House of Blues" diagonally over the forestage. A polished hardwood dance floor with inlaid strip lighting replaced the 1990's parquetry. Black hardwearing carpet covered the stage and new LED lighting replaced the old-school PARs. The smell of fresh paint and new carpet pleased Pat; he hadn't thought it possible to erase the stench of stale booze, urine, and vomit. Raffi had transformed the old club back to its former position as the flagship of Rooney's Entertainment Venues.

****

"Son, you've done well. It looks good."

"Thanks, Dad." High praise from Pat Rooney, he didn't deal in superlatives.

"Have you found a band?"

"Come, I'll show them to you."

When Raffi had sifted through Dylan's paperwork he'd found a well prepared promo for a band. When he went to their Youtube channel, he grew excited. He had envisioned himself running a week of auditions searching for a band. If still available, Mia and the Modes just landed a job.

He watched Pat's face as the first song began and said nothing. He waited; two more songs and his father leaned back in the chair.

"They're your band. Have you talked to them yet?"

"Not yet."

"Better hurry up, a band like that will get snatched up pretty quick I would imagine."

"Yeah, I'll give them a call."

20

Mia stood beside the pile of earth that covered Julie Colter. She, her boyfriend Christopher, her band mates, Luke, Matt, and Tom, and the priest who gave a short sermon were the only mourners at Julie's burial. The priest had left, and the others had retreated to the cemetery gates to wait. Mia had to insist Christopher go too, she wanted a moment alone and he persisted in his desire to stay close. He relented and went to the gates to wait. Mia knew what motivated him, jealousy of her male band mates and a need to prove his superior position in her life.

A butterfly fluttered around the flowers she had placed on the unmarked grave. She swore as soon as she could afford it, she would have a headstone erected, like those of her grandfather's, Rosie's, and Lily's graves nearby. The card tied to the bouquet, with the carefully written inscription she had made the night before, would serve as an epitaph until then.

Mia turned from the grave and moved towards the gates. She had mixed feelings about Christopher's presence at the funeral; he had showed little understanding during her grandmother's illness and resented the amount of time she had spent with her remaining relative. Her relationship with her boyfriend sped downhill, she no longer liked him—she had never loved him. He had grown as demanding as her best friend, Ashleigh. Christopher wanted her to take the next step, and in the week since her grandmother's death, the pressure increased.

"You're the only one of our group who is still a virgin, Mia. Aren't you even curious about sex?"

"Of course I am, but I want to be completely sure."

"You and me have been going out for two years, why aren't you sure? What's wrong—don't you think I'm good enough."

Mia didn't answer, she feared to concede the truth.

As she moved into the adult world, her friends—including Christopher—trailed in her wake. Binge drinking, pill popping just some of their reckless behaviour.

Most of her friends couldn't say where they planned to be in three years; Mia could clearly see the path ahead, she wanted to be a successful musician, and she put in a lot of time working on her sound, studying the masters—old and new—of her chosen field.

Out of loyalty, she stayed around her old friends but grew increasingly grateful for her band. Without them, she'd have nobody who cared about her dreams. They formed the year before and developed a firm friendship. She shared a house with Luke and Matt. Tom, the drummer, was older than the rest of the band. Married, he held a day job but loved being a part of Mia and the Modes. An experienced musician, he encouraged the younger members when they bemoaned their lack of success.

"You okay girl?" Tom put his arm around her shoulders as she emerged from the ornate cemetery gate. Christopher's sullen eyes fixed on Tom's arm.

Mia nodded, tears stood in her eyes, the enormity of her situation foremost in her mind.

"You will, Mia. One day at a time for a while, hey?"

"Yes. Thanks, Tom. One day at a time."

Tom smiled. "Maybe you will be the next Georgie Angel!"

"If only."

"Never say never…"

They drove in Tom's van to the storage sheds and picked up Julie's only remaining possessions. When she took them home, she stacked the totes in the corner of her bedroom. She didn't think she could face looking at family photos and mementos right after she buried her grandmother.

21

On Friday night, Lloyd Beaufort drove his Maserati into his father's drive. He usually visited on Saturday morning. Lloyd's mother had died ten years before and his seventy-five-year-old father, Jim Beaufort, had retired and had spent the years since, travelling.

"Dad?"

Lloyd's father watched a Game of Thrones DVD in the living room, and Lloyd flopped on the couch beside him. He had bad news for his father but waited until he finished watching the episode.

Lloyd braced himself. "Dad, I have some news."

His father's gaze turned and Lloyd watched the trepidation steal across his face.

"You do?"

"I'm sorry, Dad. Julie died ten days ago. I only know because I have a client in a hospice. I was there today to get her signature and quite by accident I saw the report of Julie's death on a nurse's desk. It's definitely our Julie, I asked the doctor in charge. She'd apparently had emphysema."

Lloyd watched the tears brim in Jim's eyes. Lloyd's sister, Julie, never got along with her family; she had left home at the age of sixteen and moved in with her boyfriend, Kerry Colter. They last heard of their eldest child thirty-two years ago when an acquaintance saw her leaving The Blacktown Hospital with Colter and a newborn baby. In spite of their attempts to contact her, the Beauforts had had no further news of their daughter. When Lloyd's mother died, he had sent Julie a letter at her last known address but she didn't come to the funeral. His parents knew nothing of their grandchild, a boy or girl they never discovered nor if that child had any siblings.

"I've got my assistant looking into her life. He's going to try and get a copy of the birth certificate of your grandchild. I'm going to find him—or her—don't worry."

"Where is she buried?"

"At Blacktown, we'll go out there tomorrow, Dad."

Lloyd put his arms around his father as he watched the tears spill from his blue eyes. Jim Beaufort's greatest regret was the estrangement of his daughter, and he'd silently grieved for the grandchild he had never met. Nothing would make him happier than to find his daughter's child. Lloyd regretted he would never give his father grandchildren. Jim had long ago accepted his son's homosexuality. Lloyd and his partner Danny didn't want children. A respected criminal lawyer, his law firm, Beaufort, Jones, and associates was among the best in Sydney.

According to what he'd learned from her death report, Julie had died with only enough money to cover a cheap funeral. Why had she subjected herself to such poverty when her family had moderate wealth? Lloyd himself was well off; he would have happily helped his sister out.

****

The next morning they arrived at the cemetery and using a map, Lloyd navigated to his sister's grave. A pile of freshly dug earth marked Julie's grave, on it, a wilting bunch of handpicked flowers tied with a piece of red ribbon threaded through a handmade card. Lloyd lifted the flowers to examine the card.

'Here lies Julie Colter, wife of Kerry and loving mother of Lily and Rosalie. I love you with all my heart, Nanna and I will miss you forever. Love Mia.'

"Dad! Look at this!"

Jim read the card then read it again.

"She has two daughters and a granddaughter."

"They shouldn't be too hard to find." Lloyd glanced at the head stone of the neighbouring grave and looked again—Kerry John Colter. "Dad, look. It's Kerry, he died seventeen years ago."

While his father read the epitaph, Lloyd examined other graves around and his heart sank. The two nieces he'd never met lay buried beside their parent's. Lloyd didn't think he would ever see a more saddened sight as he looked upon the graves of this young family and wondered what could have gone wrong:

'Rosalie Susanne Colter, beloved daughter of Julie and Kerry, sister of Lily and mother of Mia. 1982 – 1995. Aged fourteen.' The headstone beside it read, *'Lillian Anne Colter, beloved daughter of Julie and Kerry, sister of Rosalie and Aunt of Mia. 1989 – 2008. Aged nineteen.'*

"That leaves only Mia," tears fell from his father's eyes as he read the last headstone. "We have to find her, Lloyd."

"We'll find her Dad."

22

Days passed and Mia came to terms with her grandmother's death. She avoided Christopher and Ashleigh; she could not face them at this painful juncture in her life. Each day she went to her corner in the Mall and spent hours busking. Playing her guitar and singing helped her to forget her situation.

As she played she monitored the time, she needed another twenty dollars to cover her rent and her phone bill. The shops would close in another forty-five minutes. People passed, some stopped to listen, others hurried, many tossed coins into her guitar case—occasionally a note of small denomination would fall in. As she played her last few songs for the night, a tall, slender man with curly dark hair dropped a fifty-dollar note into her guitar case and moved away to lean on a lamppost; hands stuffed in his pockets, he stood and listened. Mia groaned as Christopher sauntered along the mall and leaned against the wall beside her, waiting for her to finish. As she put her guitar in its case a pair of feet caught her attention. She looked up.

"Mia?"

She stood. The fifty dollar donor towered over her.

"Yes, I'm Mia, thank you for the fifty."

"I've enjoyed listening to you. Your guitar player told me I'd find you here."

"Oh."

"A few months ago you left your band's bio at Dylan's Blues Club—"

"Oh—but—"

"It's okay. Your guitar player also told me what Dylan did. He's no longer running the club. I'm Raffi Cheney, the new manager." He shook her hand and smiled. "I've listened to your Youtube videos, and I like your sound. I want you guys as my resident band."

"Really? When can we start?"

"On Tuesday night."

"Tuesday?" Only five days away.

"Yeah—sorry about the short notice. Can you manage Tuesday?"

"Yes, of course!" Mia resisted bouncing on the spot.

He stepped closer and passed her a business card. His fingers brushed hers as she took it, his warmth pushed inside her chest. His eyes were black as moonlit shadows.

"You can come in on the weekend for a sound check and to get set up. Give me a call, I'll be there, I don't have a life."

How could you not have a life? Surely, there are women clamouring for your attention.

"Okay, I look forward to it."

"Thanks." He smiled and grazed her upper arm.

Mia shivered as he strode away.

"And who was he?"

"Nobody, Chris."

"Ready to go?"

"Go where?"

"Wherever you want."

"I'm going home, Chris, I'm tired. It's been a tough week."

"Why—what's been tough?"

"Oh not much, just my last living relative died—not much at all."

"Yeah—sorry about that."

Mia opened and shut her mouth. What could she say to such monumental insensitivity?

Is it just my generation or does every generation have its apathetic dipshits?

"I'll talk to you later, Chris." Mia walked away, grateful at least he had the nous to let her go.

****

Raffi had spent the afternoon talking to his staff; he outlined what he expected of them and told them his plans for the club. He organised the rosters, handing out and collecting tax declaration forms and employment details. He sat with Frankie, drinking beer and discussing the coming week. His uncle had agreed to fill in as bar manager until the café upstairs was ready. The back door slammed and he waited to see who had entered.

Dylan emerged, looking disgruntled.

"Raffi, I need a drink—badly."

"Sure, help yourself."

"Hey, Frankie." Dylan gave Frankie a haunted smile and pushed open the service door at the end of the bar. "What's happening?"

"Back in the service, Dylan."

"What, here?"

"Yep."

"That's good." Dylan's words came automatically; he didn't appear to be listening.

"You're looking a little frazzled, Dylan."

"Hmm? Ah yeah. Fuck it." He tossed back a nip of rum and then poured another.

"Do you plan on getting smashed?" Raffi watched another nip of rum disappear down Dylan's throat. "You never used to drink so much, Dylan. What's the deal?"

Dylan grimaced as he swallowed the burning spirit. He coughed and croaked, "My mother and brother are the deal—pair of arseholes."

Raffi looked at Frankie and raised an eyebrow; Frankie scratched behind his ear and lowered his gaze. Raffi knew Frankie shared his hatred of Dylan's mother and brother.

"Ollie has booked a table for sixteen on opening night."

"Really?" As Dylan took a seat he glowered from Raffi to Frankie, "You should have told the slimy cunt you were booked out."

"I need bums on seats, Dylan—VIP bums are better than normal bums when it comes to making the place look good."

"Trust me, Raffi, Ollie's bum ain't so fancy when it's uncovered."

"Well, as long as he keeps it covered I'll have no complaints."

"My family weren't always so high in society you know."

Frankie straightened, his head swivelled to Dylan, he scrutinized him a moment; Raffi watched as his uncle gradually relaxed.

"Old Shirley was a just a hooker until she married Pat. Ollie should be fucking grateful to Pat for supporting him through university. He only just scraped a pass in political science—oxymoron if ever I heard one. Political science, my arse." Dylan took a mouthful of his drink.

"Now he's so high in society it might give him a nosebleed; he'd be less than nobody if Shirley hadn't ensnared Pat. Seriously, Raffi, I don't know why Pat didn't marry Antoinette years ago."

Raffi chewed his lip and shook his head.

Frankie grinned. "I dressed Ollie's salad for him a few times when I was a young apprentice."

"You did? High five!" Dylan's face split happily as his palm slapped Frankie's.

"What?" Raffi looked from one man to the other. "Did I miss something?"

Frankie and Dylan giggled like schoolgirls.

"Anyway, here's to the city of Bundaberg and the finest Queensland rum." Dylan raised his glass and brought it to his lips.

****

"Hey Kate, what's happening?"

"Dylan. You're back."

And about bloody time you two-timing arsehole.

Kate had thrown her husband out two months before when she had caught him behind the stage banging a naked cocktail waitress against the wall. She let him in the front door along with a cloud of alcohol fumes.

"I've come to get some of my stuff, but if you run and clean your teeth, I'll let you suck my dick."

Kate wanted to cry. She had hoped he would have returned sooner, asking her forgiveness, but she could see he hadn't changed. She swore Dylan wanted women to hate him—he treated them as sex objects. Was it self-hatred she saw in her estranged husband?

"I hear Pat sacked you." Her heart hurt with loneliness but she refused to let him see her pain. "Not before time either."

"Did he sack you too?"

Kate followed as he strode the length of the hallway to the cupboard and began rifling through the contents. Dylan Delaney, the most attractive man she had ever met, he'd moved in with her only a month after she took the position of secretary and cashier of Dylan's Blues Club; they had married three months later. She loved him, but for the last few years of their marriage, he had taken to drinking heavily and he had treated her with nothing but disrespect. He had regarded his position as manager of the club as his ticket to free booze and sex with any woman who took his fancy.

"No. I still have my job. I must say your little brother is a much better manager than you are. He's better looking too."

"Forget it Kate, you're not his type."

"What would you know about it?"

"Ah, here it is." Dylan took out a photo album and dropped it flat on the floor. "What would I know about what?" His head deep in the cupboard.

"Oh forget it—you're too drunk to talk. I'm sick of the sight of you already."

"No you're not. You want me to fuck you." He pulled out a shoebox and sat it on top of the photo album. "I can smell it."

"Tuh! Not likely."

"I haven't got time right now. Ask me again tomorrow."

"Just hurry up and get out of my house!"

Dylan's feline movement surprise Kate—she knew he was well pissed—in one fluid turn, he spun and shoved her against the wall and hitched her skirt. His mouth crushed hers and his fingers slipped into her panties, probing and rubbing. "No, don't!" she gasped.

"You want it." He leaned in and nibbled her erect nipple through her T-shirt. "Unfortunately, my darling wife, I haven't got time."

Kate's legs shook and she tried to disguise her ragged breathing.

"Fuck off, Dylan!"

"Nah, I'll fuck you tomorrow if I get into the club early enough."

"I said fuck off! I'm not interested."

He pressed her against the wall and licked her mouth. He nibbled her lips. There was something oddly arousing in the alcohol fumes he breathed into her mouth.

"Then why is your cunt drooling for me?" He smiled and licked his fingers.

"Just go!" Kate wanted to cry. She wanted him, but it had to be on her terms.

Dylan picked up the photo album and the shoebox, his indigo eyes roamed down her body. He left her with a wink and a smack of his lips.

23

Raffi arrived a little late on Monday morning, a weekend's preparation meant a day of last minute spitting and polishing. Tuesday night the club would open its doors to the public but the official opening would be Saturday—he had four nights to ensure everything ran smoothly. He aimed to attract a higher class of patrons than Dylan had. He wanted the white-collar workers, business people, doctors, solicitors—the middle and upper class. He hoped it would work. Raffi congratulated himself on his choice of house band, Mia and the Modes. They had spent Sunday afternoon with a film crew preparing a video for a planned advertising campaign. Mia had just turned nineteen. She and her band mates in their mid to late twenties played the blues with maturity beyond their years, Raffi had spent three years working from Chicago, down the Mississippi, to

New Orleans in clubs and bars; he knew how a blues band should sound. Slim, pretty, with dark hair and indigo eyes, Mia's talent would hold the audience's attention. People would soon get bored with beauty in the absence of ability. Raffi fancied her, but he would not rush into anything. He knew the time he'd spent in prison left him inclined to grab the first pretty girl who came along. His one-night-stand with Tiffany had eased the urgency—the need to get his rocks off—but he hadn't gone back for seconds. No, he'd wait. He didn't want to frighten Mia off—she seemed sad. She smiled the sweetest smile, but it was fleeting.

Raffi shoved the office door open and caught a sight he would never un-see if he lived a hundred years. Dylan's hairy arse gyrating between a pair of legs he assumed belonged to Kate.

"Oh for fuck's sake, Dylan!"

"Raffi!" his brother puffed, "I'll be with you in a minute, Bro!"

"No, you'll be out of my fucking club in a minute, Bro. If you're not, I'll throw you out."

Raffi closed the door, went to the coffee shop across the street and bought a double shot. He was mostly immune to other people's sex scenes; he witnessed plenty of male on male action in El Rodeo. He'd been embarrassed to excruciation the first time he woke in the night to the sounds of his cell mates—three of them—going at it. Irish Ian, a red haired Irish national serving a life sentence, pumping the arse of a slim young Mexican who in turn sucked a Venezuelan cock.

The United Nations in action.

Raffi had planted his arse firmly against the wall, and wished he'd had a pillow to block the grunts and moans.

Raffi had survived two years without feeling the need to indulge himself with his prison mates. Plenty had tried to corner him and he used his size to fight them off. If that failed, he drew his gun on them; the gun he had only disposed of down the road from the *Francisco de Orellano Airport in El Coca.*

When Raffi returned to the club, Dylan looked sweaty but satisfied; Kate had disappeared.

"Sorry Bro, Kate has been pining for some hot cock; I was just doing my duty as her husband."

"Well, why didn't you do it at home?"

"I don't live with Kate anymore, she threw me out."

"Well, get her to take you back."

"What and give up my freedom? Fuck that."

"Look, I've got work to do, Dylan, so can you fuck off?"

Dylan gazed at his stepbrother, his eyes narrowed.

"Did you get any action in that gulag you were in?"

"There were no women in there, so no. I didn't."

"You didn't try any—"

"No, I didn't. Now fuck off—no wait, I have a job for you."

"Doing what?"

"Bar manager."

"I thought Frankie was doing that."

"Temporarily—I need someone permanent."

"I'll think about it."

"Well don't think too long—I need someone now."

Dylan grinned and flipped him a casual salute. "See you on opening night, little brother."

"I'd rather you didn't." Raffi didn't mean it; he liked Dylan and wished he would pull himself together. "Unless you're here to work—"

Raffi stared at the empty space Dylan left and sighed. *Better luck next time.*

24

Raffi praised his staff's performance, he'd kept as many of Dylan's staff as possible; they knew the place and he deemed it wise to take advantage of their experience. He had them all on notice, new management—new rules and if they didn't comply then they could find a new job. He had employed good-looking staff, both women and men. Raffi surprised himself with his own performance; while inside El Rodeo, he'd learned the art of diplomacy and if he could grease his way to friendship with a thousand murderous Latin American prisoners, he could easily win the esteem of a club full of Sydney-siders. He moved among the patrons with ease, getting to know people and seeing to their satisfaction with the service. Buy a round of drinks here and there—give the big parties their own private drink waiter. He made good use of Dylan—seeing he couldn't convince him to stay away—he got him to point out the rich socialites, the who's who of Sydney society, then he made a point of flirting with the women and talking deferentially to the wealthy business people. Let them think he valued their opinions and advice; some of it he did value—but not all. He found himself good at listening as some old fart rattled on about the secret to his success. He had always been an expert at remembering people's names and achieved first name terms with many he hoped would be regulars. Raffi knew the secret to his own success would involve getting his customers to spend up. The place was booked out for the official opening—all the tables reserved. Any extras who showed up on the night would have to stand at the bar.

"Hey Raff!" Dylan came up beside him, three sheets to the wind and sailing. "Who's the little darling playing the piano?"

You ought to know you lecherous arsehole, given you manhandled her the last time you saw her.

"Nobody that should concern you, Dylan."

"Ah-hah! Raffi's got his eye on the singer!"

"Maybe I have—maybe I haven't. But if you put one greasy finger on her I'll rip it right off. Okay?"

"Well if you're not going to fuck her—"

"She is my employee; keep your filthy paws off her and all my female staff." Raffi knew his older brother regarded his female staff as a smorgasbord of tits and arse.

"What about Kate?"

"She's your wife, do what you like, but do it elsewhere. I never want to see your hairy arse going at it in my office again. Ah shit—"

Tiffany sauntered down the steps with a group of friends; he wanted people to come but not her. He'd had a good time with her for a few hours but he had no inclination to go there again. Several women had already dragged him onto the dance floor. It went with the job—let them think he found them attractive—they'd be back again next week. He'd danced with them for one song and then excused himself on the pretext of needing to supervise the goings on behind the bar.

"Raffi!"

"Hello, Tiffany. Nice of you to drop by my club."

Now fuck off.

"It's a pleasure. These are my friends, Sara, Deb, Jay, and Jamie." She leaned close to his ear and her companions surged forward to greet Raffi, shaking his hand and congratulating him on his club.

The hair on the back of his neck prickled when Sara shouted over the music, "Tiffany has told us all about you."

"Hm. Excuse me, I have to be over there." Raffi nodded towards the bar and sped across the crowded room, weaving through the sweaty, well-dressed bodies. A group of minor celebrities waylaid him halfway to the bar. Massey Moran, a radio shock-jock grabbed his arm and Raffi had no option but to shake his hand. He reminded himself he must be sociable and take their gushing in his stride. Two female TV journalists accompanied Massey; he introduced them as Jackie and Kellie.

"Raffi, you must come into the station one morning and I'll interview you, the publicity would be great for us both."

"Um—yeah—I'll have a think about it. I need publicity for my club, but not for myself."

"I bet you have some enthralling tales to tell."

"Yeah—but I don't think I'll be telling them anytime soon. Sorry Massey, but it's a little premature."

"If you require a biographer, Raffi, let me know." The female journalist named Jackie handed him a business card.

"Sure, maybe one day." He gave her his best smile and slipped the card in his pocket with at least ten others handed to him that evening. He looked back towards the stage and caught Tiffany in his line of sight, pouting in his direction. He sighed, he screwed her once, what more did she want?

No good deed goes unpunished—or so they say.

"Maybe I will take you up on a small interview, Massey, along with an advertising campaign."

Take advantage of every situation, Raffi.

"Call my people, Raffi!"

"I will."

He caught Frankie's eye and gave him a 'save me' look. Frankie grinned and beckoned him to the bar.

"Excuse me, people—duty calls. Nice meeting you, I hope to see you here again sometime."

When Mia and the Modes took the stage, the room was half-full. Mia hoped the crowd would increase. She loved performing with her band; it was much easier than busking with an acoustic guitar. Her confidence increased with the crowd. Raffi gave her a smile and the thumbs up from where he spoke to a group of patrons and she almost forgot the words to the song she sang. Ashleigh, Christopher, and a group of their mutual friends appeared halfway through the night, and Mia would have ground her teeth but the middle of a verse of Pride and Joy prevented it. They didn't belong in a blues club; they didn't appreciate the music and their hipster clothing came off odd. While on a break, Mia sought Raffi out to get some feedback. She only managed three words.

"What do you—?"

"Mia! I love this place! It's so cool!" Ashleigh threw her arms around Mia and hugged her tight. "And who is your handsome friend?"

"Raffi, these are my friends, Ashleigh, Christopher, Toni and…" Christopher made a show of putting his arm around Mia and pulling her close, he didn't acknowledge Raffi. Toni waved her fingers at Raffi and turned her attention back to the DJ in his booth beside the stage.

"Mia! Why didn't you tell me this place was run by a male model?"

Raffi's brow creased at Ashleigh and Mia winced. Ashleigh appeared to have already had too much to drink.

"Why do you play all that weird music, Mia?" Toni's taste in music ranged from hip-hop to Top of the Pops, Mia doubted she had heard of the Blues.

"It's not weird, Toni—it's just beyond your mental capacity."

"You should sing some Beyoncé; you have the voice for it."

Mia swallowed the frosty retort that burned her tongue. It served her best interest to keep people coming back to this club; even airheads spend money over the bar. A tall blonde sidled up to Raffi and spoke in his ear and he shook his head. Mia never caught what she said but Ashleigh apparently had.

"No! Raffi's going to dance with me, aren't you Raffi?" She moved in and tried to wrap her arms around him.

"Um, no—actually, I have things to do."

The blonde gave Ashleigh a wilting flash of her almond eyes. "Do go away, you irritating little Hobbit!"

"Don't call me a Hobbit, I'll kick your fat arse all over King's Cross, Bitch!" Ashleigh planted her fists on her hips.

"Oh! Get rid of the strap-on and accept it—you're an insignificant little cretin."

"Watch it bitch, I'll…"

Mia cringed as Raffi's mouth twitched with repressed laughter.

"…that I promise with all my heart!" Ashleigh laid her fist across her chest.

"Your heart? That little yellow thing buried under an inch of chest hair?"

"Now calm down ladies." Raffi held a small device, a stun gun Mia hoped. The blonde and Ashleigh threw insult-grenades back and forth. The blonde's acidic tongue fascinated Mia. It intrigued her how someone could deliver such an effortless tirade of bitchiness—Ashleigh was out of her depth.

A brawny security stepped up to Raffi's side.

"You buzzed, Raff?"

"Take these two girls and read them the riot act. If they don't accept the terms of entry, they can leave."

Mia watched the security man lead Ashleigh and the blonde away towards the main entrance.

"Ooh! I thought Ashleigh was going to punch that chick!" Toni's eyes widened, "she was—"

"Excuse me, but I need to talk to Mia, alone." Raffi took Mia's arm and pulled her out of Christopher's grip. As he led her away, she worried he might be angry with her for attracting such a dumb crowd. He led her up the stairs to the foyer lounge and sat down in a dimly lit corner.

"I hope you didn't mind me dragging you away like that," he smiled. "Is Christopher your boyfriend?"

"No—yeah—I don't know—"

Raffi grinned. "I'll take that as no then."

"He's serious but I—well." Mia shrugged.

"Your friends are kind of irritating. Ashleigh is an idiot."

"But that other woman was kind of nasty too."

He grinned. "She's got a mouth on her."

"Is she your girlfriend?"

"Hell no!"

"I'm sorry Ashleigh did that. I think she's had too much to drink."

"Are they your close friends?"

"Yes and no. Ashleigh used to be my best friend."

"Why do you keep them around?"

"I don't know—they are friends from my high school days but I don't have much in common with them anymore. I agree they are a pain."

Raffi caressed her cheek with the back of his fingers. "You've outgrown them, Mia."

"I guess I have."

"Come, I'll buy you a drink. You're doing a fantastic job up there, by the way."

25

People packed wall to wall in Raffi's House of Blues. The door attendants had permission to overcrowd by sixty people. It is a strange thing about people—crowds attract crowds and on opening night, a wise manager will take the chance and overcrowd, then pray like mad the fire department won't decide to come inspecting.

The socialites and their ilk—those who wanted exposure had booked the large tables along the centre of the room. The staff in their white shirts, black trousers and bow ties, cruised among the patrons delivering drinks and trays of hors d'oeuvres. Pretty waitresses dodged the groping hands of the sleazes and the young waiters smiled as they suffered the attention of the cougars. The rubber matting behind the bar grew wet and sticky as the harried staff found no downtime keeping up with demand. The young, unknown band proved popular. People sent texts telling their friends about their new favourite band, Mia and the Modes. Phone screens dotted the crowd as revellers filmed and took selfies, each message sent from those on the dance floor wreaked havoc with the sound system.

****

The mixer operator in his booth above the stairs sweated and cursed. He took pleasure in mixing for Mia and the Modes; they kept their onstage volume at a controllable level and trusted the soundman to handle the front of the house. He'd be kicking goals except for those cursed phones.

First world problems. More ferrite chokes on the cables is what I need.

He raked the back of his neck and took a long slurp from his beer.

****

Overseeing the staff had kept Raffi busy for the first three hours, making sure everyone did their job. Now he had time to relax and socialise. He stopped at his parent's table and got a firm stamp of approval from his father.

"Well done, Raff—I couldn't have set this joint up better if I tried."

It meant a lot to Raffi to have his father's approval.

"Thanks, Dad."

"You've packed them in, I noticed."

"Nah—only to regulation, Dad—plus sixtyish."

Pat grinned and gave him the thumbs up. "An extra sixty people will bring in at least three grand over the bar. Worth the risk unless you get caught."

"I'm used to taking risks."

The DJ began his set as Mia and the Modes took a break. Raffi made to rise, he wanted to talk to Mia—he had no good excuse—but the more time he spent with her the happier he was. Dylan stumbled past in the direction of the stage.

"Hey, Dylan!"

Dylan stopped and looked around.

"Hey, little brother!"

"Are you okay, Dylan?"

"Never better, Raff—never better." Dylan crouched down beside Raffi's chair and leaned heavily on his thigh. "'M lookin' for—urp—for Kate, have you seen her?"

"I think she went home, mate. She didn't intend to stay late."

"I think—urh! I think I might have fucked up where Kate is c—hic—concerned."

"It's not too late to do something about it."

Dylan wasn't listening, his eyes narrowed as they fixed on something across the room. Raffi followed his gaze and settled on his step-brother, Oliver Jackson, seated at the biggest table in the middle of the room he had Mia by the wrist and a smarmy smile on his face.

****

Mia had to stop several times on her way to the bar. People wanted to talk—request a song—compliment her performance—advise her to audition for Australia's Got Talent. She had grown used to it since Tuesday night. Her first residential gig involved taking time to talk to the patrons. Many people wouldn't know a good band if it set up in their ear and played Chuck Berry like a boss, but they appreciated a friendly greeting and conversation, being an entertainer demanded it. Half way down the room a man beckoned her to his table.

"So, do you like playing in my father's nightclub?"

"Y—Your father?" Mia looked around; the man didn't introduce himself or ask her name.

"Pat Rooney is my father. Not many people know that."

"Oh—I see." Mia still didn't know his name and Pat being his father left her none the wiser.

"I don't think the girl knows who you are, Oliver," said a woman across the table.

"Perhaps she votes for the other party." The man sitting beside her raised a cynical eyebrow.

"I'm Oliver Jackson." He shook her hand with a muscular grip and didn't release it; he gained a better hold by grasping her wrist with his other hand.

"Oh, it's nice to meet you, Mr Jackson." He pulled her to stand a little too close for comfort.

"I think I'll have my birthday party here next month and you can sing me happy birthday. How does that sound?"

"Um—nice. Sure, I can do that."

But how about you let go of my hand you slimy bastard!

Dylan made Mia uncomfortable but his brother creeped her out. Dylan seemed a happy drunk—a little too fond of cuddling every woman who crossed his path. Oliver had a scary manner. She pulled back trying to free her hand but he held on, she could feel the circulation dwindling in her fingers.

A hand grasped Oliver's wrist and squeezed. Mia looked up to see Dylan, his face dark with anger.

"Let her go or I'll break your girly wrist."

A brief flash of anger rippled across Oliver's face, replaced with a sudden smile.

"Hey little brother, how are they hanging?"

"Yours won't be hanging at all if you touch her again, they'll be stuffed up your miserable arse."

"Hey, I was just being friendly—"

“Come on, Mia.” Raffi appeared at her side and drew her away. “You really don’t want to get tangled up in their family fights.”

“He’s a bit of a Klingon isn’t he?”

“Nah—Ferengi. Come on, let’s get a drink.”

26

Kate appreciated that Raffi didn't comment on the scene he'd walked in on. She hadn't intended to let Dylan have his way with her; not right there in the office. But Dylan always had his way, with any woman he fancied. He seduced them, screwed then disrespected them, his looks and charm gave him latitude. Everyone liked Dylan—unless you happened to be one of those he had disrespected.

As she walked through the nightclub towards the loading dock, she slowed to watch as Raffi, dressed in board shorts and no shirt, stacked chairs, preparing to vacuum the floor. She admired his work ethic; he and his mother cleaned the nightclub every day to save money while he grew the business. Dylan had done nothing in his last few years as manager. Nothing except screw the female staff and drink copious quantities of rum from the bar. In Kate's opinion, Pat Rooney had made a mistake when he gave management of the club to Dylan. With freakish timing, Raffi arrived home, gaunt and prison scarred looking for a job. Three weeks after Kate had thrown him out Dylan had gone on one of his famous benders, he had disappeared for two weeks and Pat reached the end of his tether.

Raffi turned and grinned at her as she passed. He favoured his mother's family in looks—curly black hair and spectacular dark eyes; he barely resembled Pat Rooney, but he had his father's no nonsense manner when doing business. He looked older than twenty-four; prison life had hardened the boy who'd left Australia six years before.

Kate continued past the stage and out to the back dock; she needed to check on some stock in the storeroom. As she stepped in, she flicked on the light and gasped.

"What are you—?" She fumbled as she tried to pull the door back open but only succeeded in latching it.

Her husband had Cerise, the cocktail waitress naked across a pile of boxes. Kate froze and wondered if Raffi knew the goings on in the storeroom. Cerise worked a day shift to help organise the cold-rooms.

"Can't you go somewhere else and do that?"

Dylan opened his fly and released his erection. Even hurt and embarrassed, it quietly amazed Kate he could get it up when so drunk.

"I thought you might want some but you were too busy. Wouldn't you love what she's getting, Kate?"

"Not interested."

"Yes, you are."

Kate couldn't look away as he thrust hard, the girls breasts bounced and she moaned as he tweaked her nipples. Dylan pushed her legs up to rest on his shoulders, Kate backed out the door and her heart bound as the couple came together, she stumbled away, choking on her tears.

"Why can't I hate him?" she whispered.

****

Grennie Barnes smiled. He could have done something to keep Kate from going into the dry store but his devious nature held back. Grennie had a penchant for spreading misery.

Raffi's House of Blues, my arse!

He had stayed working for Pat Rooney on Shirley's orders. He'd been waiting for her to give him some instructions to bring Rooney to his knees, Grennie lacked the imagination to devise his own plan. He began working for Pat Rooney at seventeen, as a kitchen hand and storeman. He'd continued working for Pat, going wherever the boss sent him but for the last few years he'd been working in this club. As he watched Dylan slowly drag it downhill, he'd hoped Pat would give him the management position but young Raffi had slid in on a shrimp sandwich. Grennie had arrived for work to find a tall thin young man in control.

"Who the fuck are you?" He had asked. The last time he had seen Rafael Cheney, he was a scrawny twelve-year old. Now he towered over Grennie and had a dangerous look about him.

"I'm your new boss, now get in there and clean out the mess in that dry store."

Grennie would have told him to shove it, but he'd just bought a new car and needed a job. Grennie used to help himself at every opportunity, but with Raffi running the joint like a well-oiled machine, Grennie didn't dare nick any booze or stick his fingers in the till. Instead, he bided his time. One day he'd get even with Pat Rooney.

27

Mia wiped the dust off her piano and sniffed.

"Blah! What's that smell?"

"Smells like a pair of old socks," said Tom.

Mia wrinkled her nose and sniffed again. "Ugh!"

Sunday morning, she and her band had arrived at the club to tidy the stage and adjust the equipment. They'd let themselves in the back door but hadn't seen anyone about. Mia guessed Raffi was in his office. She gave a startled yelp when something cold and wet touched the back of her bare leg.

"Sid! Come here you old pervert!" Raffi poked his head out of the service door at the end of the main bar. "Nic!"

Mia looked around to see an old Labrador sniffing her leg and wagging his tail. He began to puff loudly and his face split into a slobbery grin. A boy about nine-years old, boy version of Raffi, ran up the steps of the stage.

"Sorry," he said. "Sid, come here." He grabbed to dog by the collar and dragged him away. "Sorry."

A smaller boy jogged behind, chewing his thumb knuckle; he too bore a strong resemblance to Raffi.

Mia smiled at them. "It's okay, he just gave me a fright."

"I'm sorry for the bad smell," the older boy grinned, "He found a dead rat in the laneway."

"Tie him up out in the loading dock, Nic." Raffi spoke from close beside her. "Sorry, Sid is pretty obnoxious." He smiled down at her and she noticed the scars on his cheeks. She wanted to touch but remembered her place.

"W—we were wondering about the smell."

"He smells like—" Raffi stopped. "Um—like the back streets of Caracas."

"I went backpacking through there once." Tom diffused the tension.

"Yeah, so did I." Raffi gave them a haunted smile. He touched Mia on the arm. "Come and see me before you go, I've got to pay you guys for the week."

"So, are you sure you're happy with us?" Mia asked.

"Very happy. Play like that every week and you'll have a job for life."

Mia watched him step down from the stage and stride back to the bar. The two little boys ran and fell into step beside him; they asked an endless barrage of questions. When she first met Raffi, the attraction was instant. The absence of a wedding ring gave her hope, but now—seeing those little boys hopping along beside him, worshipping him—it disappointed her. The boys had to be his, they favoured him and if he had sons, then a woman must surely lurk in the background. It worried her; she had seen warmth in his black eyes, and on more than one occasion, he had shown an interest. If she fell in love with Raffi, it would be her first love. Falling in love with an unavailable man would be a disaster.

Two hours later Mia's hopes swung high again.

"Dad!" The little boys ran through the door to the side of the stage and out to the loading dock, they returned half a minute later. Pat Rooney carried the smaller boy and his brawny arm wrapped around Nic's shoulders.

"Where is my other son?"

"Here, Dad." Raffi's curly head popped up from behind the bar.

Mia couldn't help smile, the boys were Raffi's brothers.

****

"Mia, we're going now. Are you coming?"

Mia sat chatting with Raffi and his father; his little brothers had gone home with Raffi's uncle Frankie.

Mia got to her feet, she knew her band waited for her but she found it hard to drag herself away from Raffi's company.

"Yes—"

"Wait. I'll drive you home." Raffi reached across and grasped her arm.

"Are you sure?"

"Very." His hand warmed her skin. "After you have a drink with me."

Pat stretched his arms. "I might tootle off too, son."

"Before you go, Dad, I want to show you something."

Raffi led them up to the foyer and through a door he kept locked; up a long stairs to a top floor room and switched on the lights.

"So why are you showing me the attic, Raff?"

Mia looked around at the dusty room; she never knew there was a second floor to Raffi's House of Blues. The dusty furniture stacked along one wall almost obscured the light from the grimy windows.

"I'm going to turn this into a late night café, Dad. Or maybe even a restaurant. Frankie is interested in a partnership."

"Frankie's a good chef," said Pat.

Mia watched Pat Rooney's face as he looked around.

"You've got some cleaning ahead of you. This room hasn't been used for at least fifteen years that I know of."

"I want this place to be a complete entertainment venue, Dad. Punters can come and eat—in here or out there on the balcony, they'll have a nice view of the mall.

Then they can mosey on downstairs. I can do it. I just need to get planning permission."

"And a few million bucks more."

"Frankie said he'd throw in a few dollars; the rest I'll borrow. I estimate I'll need about two million. I'll have to install a lift, people won't like hiking up those stairs."

"And a kitchen."

"Yep—it'll be at that end, I'll get that old dumbwaiter fixed up so we can send stuff up from the back dock."

"You've thought this out, haven't you?"

"Yep, and when it's up and running I'm going to renovate the old fly-loft, make it into a cocktail lounge. It's a perfect size."

"That'll cost a fair bit too."

"It can be done—I estimate…"

Mia listened as the two men tossed around figures she could barely comprehend. Throughout her childhood, money had always been scarce. Her grandmother could barely afford Mia's piano lessons. Mia still bought most of her clothes at the op shop. The money she made playing in the club downstairs was more than she ever imagined she'd earn in a week.

"Well, let's get plans drawn up and get it approved and then we'll look at the finance."

"The plans are already in for approval." Raffi grinned. "I put it in the pipeline when the renovations begun downstairs." He moved to stand beside Mia; his hand touched hers, his fingers searching. Her stomach swooped as his hand closed around hers. As Pat wandered away to look at the doors leading to the balcony, Raffi gazed down at her. He leaned down to kiss her as Pat spoke again.

"We can open this wall right up along here."

"Hold that thought," he sighed and smiled. "Yes, that's what I'm planning, Dad."

****

"Now for that drink I said we'd have." Raffi closed the back door behind his father and clicked the lock; he turned to Mia. "One good thing about running a nightclub is easy access to the bar. Which, in the case of my predecessor wasn't a good thing."

"Dylan?"

"He completely stuffed the place because he couldn't stay out of the bar; still can't. I'm always chasing him. He's a hopeless alcoholic."

"He's your brother isn't he?"

"Stepbrother. I have two older stepbrothers. You've met the other one as well, Oliver Jackson. He's a government minister."

"Oh, him. Dylan didn't seem to like him."

"Ollie's a scumbag. Dylan is a nice bloke; he just needs to leave off the booze and the women." Behind the bar, Raffi poured their drinks; he looked back at her and smiled. "He's already screwed two of my female staff."

Mia shuddered as she remembered the big, handsome man's steely grip on her arm.

"He's married to Kate, by the way—the office lady." Raffi carried their drinks and pushed the service door open with his elbow. "They're separated."

"Poor woman."

"Anyway," he led her to the closest booth and they sat down. "Enough of my stepbrothers, I want to know about you."

"Oh. Like what?"

He smiled. "Everything. I know you're nineteen, but where are you from? Where did you grow up?"

"I'm not very interesting—"

"You are to me."

"I grew up out at Blacktown."

"Are your parents still there?"

Mia almost choked on her drink.

What parents?

"I was raised by my grandmother." She stared at the bubbles sliding up the inside of her glass.

"Oh, is she still there?"

"She died not long ago." Mia's throat tightened.

"Jesus, Mia. I didn't know. I'm sorry—" His arms wrapped around her and pulled her close. "What about the rest of your family?"

Mia shook her head and tears filled her eyes. "There are none."

"Mia, I'm sorry," Raffi drew her cheek against his neck; his lips brushed her forehead. "I ask too many questions."

"It's okay, I'm coping better now, I think."

Being close to Raffi halted her tears; she could hear his heart thumping in his chest—faster than it should beat. He tilted her face to his, the passion in his black eyes flooded her senses, time slowed as his lips found hers. His body heat stole through hers; she tingled where their hips touched—where his fingers slipped under her shirt to caress the bare skin of her waist.

"That guy you were with the other night, what do I need to do to take you away from him?"

Mia smiled, "You just did it." Mia didn't know how to tell Christopher farewell, but Raffi inspired her courage.

"Good, I'd hate to have to take you away by force."

His hand came to rest below her ear; his thumb caressed her cheek as their breaths mingled. Mia's smile dissolved as his lips warmed hers, intoxicating her and drawing her into his world.

"Are you hungry?" His mouth moved to the side of her neck.

"Yes—starving."

"Me too. I know a little fried chicken stand not far from here." He stood up and pulled her to her feet. He took a bottle of champagne and two glasses from the bar. "A night-time picnic in the park for you and me."

Along the cold, rain-soaked street, hand in hand they strolled to the fried chicken stand, the city around them fell away as he interrupted their progress to lean down and kiss her rain-bedewed lips. As they waited under the awning for their chicken, he wrapped his arm around her; Mia's heart fluttered as her body pressed against his. She sunk into the warmth of his side, her arms stole around him and she smiled, lost in his black eyes.

They sheltered from the drizzle, eating fried chicken and drinking champagne. Those hours stretched to eternity and when Raffi dropped her home Mia couldn't stop smiling. The small pearl of hope that had seeded in her breast over the past week swelled to a shining star.

28

Three weeks after she had buried her grandmother, Mia bought a wreath of roses and went to visit her grave. The midmorning sun seared the back of her neck; feet accustomed to pavement crunched and sank deep in the gravel street of this city of the dead. A city full but empty. A magpie warbled a minatory air, a warning this place belonged to him. Mia contemplated her situation. She now faced the future with a little more optimism than she had the day of her grandmother's funeral. Raffi had brought her unexpected joy and even if their relationship failed, being the lead singer of a resident band in a popular nightclub would give her status as a musician; a privilege not experienced by many nineteen-year-olds. She smiled as her thoughts circled back to Raffi; tall, thin and handsome. He had a wiry toughness and an easy, confident nature; his staff and patrons liked him. The time to end her relationship with Christopher had arrived. Mia loved Raffi and Christopher could not compete.

She turned up the path to where her family lay and for a moment, believed she had taken a wrong turn. She paused and checked the graves of her other relatives alongside, stunned at the sight of a brand-new headstone to her grandmother's grave, an inscription of Mia's epitaphic note etched into the marble. She feared approaching—how could this be? Who would pay for a headstone on the grave of a stranger? Mia touched the cool white stone; her fingers traced the black and gold inscription. She checked the grass beside the grave, it might hold clues—footprints of this anonymous benefactor.

"Who did this, Nanna?"

She set her wreath against the headstone and picked up a dozen wilting roses. A card read, 'Your father loves you, Julie.'

Father? She said her father was dead.

Mia reread the card, 'Your father loves you.'

Loves. Present tense.

Julie Colter must have had more family than she let on.

But who? Where?

Mia lingered by the grave, hoping by some miracle the stone would tell her where it came from. Hoping that person might show up. When she left, her mind buzzed with questions.

29

Mia had stored her backpack in the dressing room behind the stage when angry voices reached her. With no desire to intrude she leaned against the wall out of sight.

"That's the bloody lot, Ollie. Stop fretting. Your political career will keep sailing on, unfettered by your past indiscretions—"

"Shut up!" A hushed female voice answered.

"You may not care about your reputation, Dylan, but I care about mine," The man's voice had a serrated edge.

"You're a fucking hypocrite, Ollie."

"At least he's made something of his life, Dylan," said the woman. "Why don't you dry yourself out and find a new job."

"Fuck that, Ma. Every time I stop drinking I start remembering all that stuff—"

"Shh! Shut up!"

"I might become dangerous if I stop drinking. I might turn into a human being again, you know, grow a conscience…"

"You'll keep your mouth shut if you know what's good for you."

"I could hang you by your balls, Ollie—"

Mia heard a scuffle and the woman hissed, "Stop it! Both of you! I fixed it for you back then—don't fuck it up!"

"What do you tell your highfalutin friends when they ask you how you got the scar on your hand, Ol?"

"I'll fuckin' strangle you, you cunt—"

"Go ahead and try! The last time you beat me up I was a skinny fifteen year old; now, even pissed I could break your scrawny neck—"

"Stop it! Both of you! Now Dylan, is that all of the photos?"

"That's every last fucking photo I own, Ma. Peruse at your leisure, I've got no fucking use for them."

"It better be all—"

"Let's go Ollie, before that little French whore's bastard comes back."

"Watch it, Shirley, the little French whore might steal your meal ticket if you're not careful—in fact I think she already has."

"Don't call our mother by her first name, to us she's Mum and Pat's not her meal ticket, he's her husband."

"Really? I think he reneged on that role long ago. Ah—fuck the both of you; I like Raffi and his mother."

"Yeah? Watch your back with him, two years in jail—I wouldn't trust him as far as I can throw him."

"You watch yourself, Ol. You might get a lot worse than two—"

"Shut up!"

"Both of you stop it! Now Dylan, get yourself together. Oliver doesn't need you to spoil his good name with your drinking and carousing."

"Ah fuck off, both of you!"

Their footsteps moved off and faded. Mia trembled a little. Had Raffi really spent two years in prison? Mia had fallen in love with the manager of Raffi's House of Blues. He seemed so nice and she trusted him.

What is the secret that Dylan holds over his politician brother?

Mia took a calming breath and made her way to the stage. Monday afternoon and the boys would be here soon to run through a few songs but she first had to practice her scales; something she'd neglected since her grandmother had died.

****

"Go away, Dylan, I'm busy." In the middle of transferring staff wages, Kate looked up to see her husband leaning against the doorframe clutching a bottle of Toohey's.

"I thought you might like a quickie." His eyes held a look somewhere between anger and lust.

"I'm busy and besides, Raffi will be back in a minute."

"Ah fuck it, I'll go and see if I can crack onto the little piano player. Now there's a horny little darling if ever I saw one."

"Fuck off, Dylan."

"She's prettier than you—"

"Everyone's prettier than me in your eyes, Dylan, there's nothing I can do about it.

"You could lose a few pounds."

"And you could lose that fucking bottle!"

"That, I can't do, sweet wife."

He stumbled off and Kate brushed away furious tears.

Fuck the piano player and the dumb blond cocktail waitress—and how many others?

He only need give a woman that look and she'd fall at his feet.

****

Raffi closed the dry store, tucked the clipboard under his arm and headed for his office; he had orders to place. As he emerged into the clubroom, the sight of his stepbrother standing beside Mia, stroking her hair and trying to chat her up riled him. Mia sat at her piano and cowered.

"Dylan!" he jumped up onto the stage. "Bugger off!"

"Aw Raffi, I'm just talking to her."

Mia ducked under his arm, clinked the piano keys as she moved away.

"If you lay a finger on her again, I'll rip your fucking head off. Now I'm not going to ban you from this club, you are my brother. So far I haven't taken your key, but the next time you piss me off, that's exactly what I'll do."

"Okay, Raffi. Point taken." He stepped past Raffi and stopped for a moment in front of Mia as though he might speak but shook his head and walked away.

"Dylan, pull yourself together, please. That bar manager job is still yours—"

"Not gonna happen, little brother." He waved a dismissive hand.

"Where are you living? What—"

Dylan disappeared and left Raffi to guess. If he wasn't with Kate, he must be back under old Shirley's roof. Raffi shuddered; if there was one woman on earth he truly despised and feared, it was his father's wife.

"Are you okay, Mia?" He pulled her against him; her slim body warm and comforting.

"Yes, I'm fine. He's kind of hard to shake off, isn't he?"

"Well, as a male, I wouldn't know, he's got a bad name." Raffi touched his lips to hers; he longed to bed her but resolved he would let her set the pace for their relationship. "He listens to me. Sometimes. Hopefully he won't come near you again."

30

Late afternoon, Mia collected her backpack from the dressing room, Raffi had gone home with a promise he'd pick her up later, they had a dinner date. As she emerged from the dressing room two police officers came from the clubroom, accompanied by Kate.

"Miss Colter?" said the male officer.

"Yes?" Mia looked at the two officers and at Kate. She didn't know Kate well but thought she seemed uncomfortable.

"Would you mind if we check your bag?"

"Why?"

"Mrs Delaney believes you may have stolen a large sum of money from the manager's office."

For a moment, Mia didn't know who Mrs Delaney was, then realised they referred to Kate.

"Why would you think that?" She shook her head and handed her backpack to the female officer who opened it and pulled out a bundle of cash, secured with a rubber band.

Mia blenched. "There must be some mistake. I haven't been into the office all afternoon."

"Then where did you get this money?"

"It's not mine! I—"

"We'd like you to accompany us to the station, please, Miss Colter."

"But I didn't take it. Isn't there security cameras?"

"Strangely enough, they were turned off."

"Can I call someone?"

"You can."

Mia hesitated. She had no relatives she could call and could see no point in calling any of her band, nor Ashleigh. She'd spent the past week avoiding Christopher. Raffi was the only person who could help her. She feared what he would say or do for it was from him they accused her of stealing.

He picked up after a ring.

"Hi gorgeous, don't tell me you're going to stand me up tonight," he said.

"Raffi," she supressed a sob, she'd held it together until she heard his voice. Now the tears rolled down her cheeks. "I—"

"Hey, what's up?"

Mia's voice quavered as she told him what had happened, she finished to silence on the end of the line.

"Raffi? I never did it—please believe me!"

"I believe you, baby. I'm just trying to figure out who would put that money in your backpack."

"I don't know. I only went into the office to see you when I arrived this morning. Why would the security cameras be off?" Her throat tightened. "Raffi, I don't even know how to turn them off!"

"Mia, calm down. I'm going to call Kate and then I'll be at the station."

"Okay."

"Don't worry, you won't be charged. I know I locked the safe when I left and the only others who know how to unlock it are Dad, Kate and Dylan."

Mia sniffed back a sob and nodded.

"Mia?"

"Yes?"

"I love you, Mia."

She sobbed; the accusation against her had leached her heart of warmth, and his words gave her the comforting sense of the belonging she had craved since the death of her grandmother.

"I love you too, Raffi," she whispered.

****

Lloyd Beaufort picked up his brief case and switched off his desk lamp. His mobile buzzed in his pocket.

"Sharyn, are you still working at this late hour? You and I both need to get a life." Sharyn was a duty solicitor with an office in Lloyd's building.

"Lloyd, I'm at The Cross Police Station and they have brought in a girl called Mia Colter, that's the name of that long lost niece of yours, isn't it?"

"That's her name! Have you spoken to her?"

"No, they've taken her into an interview room."

"Are you going to be there long?" He sped out of his office and along the corridor.

"I don't think I'm going to get away from here for at least a couple of hours."

Lloyd sped into the lift and poked the button for the basement car park.

"If they release her before I get there, can you ask her to wait?"

"I'll try, Lloyd. If I see her—I have two clients to deal with"

"Thanks, Sharyn."

Lloyd ran from the lift across the carpark to his car, as soon as he started the car he voice-dialled Danny to tell him he'd be late.

Ten minutes later, he cursed the Monday evening traffic. He thought of calling his father but decided he'd first ascertain it was her. He had found an M Colter in the phone book but when he went to the address, an irritable woman in her fifties greeted him. The Mia Colter he'd found on the electoral roll no longer resided at that address and nobody knew to where she had moved. There were no cars registered to a girl of her name and age. He knew how old she was, he'd managed to get a friend who worked at the offices of Births, Deaths, and Marriages to have a look at her birth record—a long shot, but he'd hoped he might find the girl's father but the birth certificate said father unknown.

****

Raffi called Kate's number again, she didn't answer. Annoyed, he called Dylan and the number diverted.

"Shirley Jackson speaking."

Raffi's skin crawled; he hated his father's wife with a passion.

"Can I talk to Dylan Delaney, please?"

"Dylan Jackson is not here."

"Oh fuck off!" Raffi hung up. The old bitch insisted her sons use her maiden name but Raffi knew Dylan stubbornly stuck to his father's surname. Ollie had changed to Jackson when he'd begun university.

Why has nobody Burked that old bitch out with a pillow by now?

Raffi called Kate's number again.

"Kate! About bloody time you answered—what is this crap that Mia stole money from the safe?"

"The police found it in her bag."

"Who the hell put it there?"

"I assume she did."

"Who turned off the security cameras?"

"She must have."

"Bullshit, Kate! You want to get fired, or you want to tell me the truth, because so help me, I'll not only fire you, I'll kick your front teeth in."

Silence. Raffi raked his fingers through his hair.

"Look Kate, if you've planted that money on her in an effort to get rid of her, own up now. I'll understand, I will. I know Dylan has been using the girl to hurt your feelings but there is nothing going on there I assure you, Mia is my girlfriend."

Kate didn't speak.

"I'll be getting the police to fingerprint the safe and the cupboard where the camera monitors are. They'll finger print the bag the cash was in too I would imagine."

Still no sound.

"Kate? Talk to me."

"I'm sorry," she squeaked, "I thought she was Dylan's latest girlfriend; I can't stand it anymore, Raffi. I didn't know what else to do—"

"You'll call the police right now, that's what you'll do. Ah, fuck it—I'm not going to have you charged or anything, you have enough on your plate with Dylan. Look, take a week off, Kate. You must be owed some holiday time, or take compassionate leave—whatever, just take a week off and I'll try to talk to Dylan, if I can find him."

Raffi hung up and decided to walk the short distance from his unit in Rushcutters Bay. If he tried to drive at this hour it would take three times as long and then he'd need to park when he got there. Driven by newfound love, Raffi ran; Mia needed him. She was a girl with nobody to turn to except him. He couldn't imagine being nineteen and having no family. At the age of twenty-two, Raffi found himself in trouble in Venezuela, and his father had travelled half way across the world to come to his aid. Mia found herself in trouble because two people, old enough to know better, couldn't get their lives together.

The time had come for Raffi to have a long talk to his stepbrother and find out what bothered him.

<h1 style="text-align:center">31</h1>

Mia waited in the interview room for over an hour and finally a woman put her head in the door and called over her shoulder to her colleague. They entered and the woman dropped a file on the desk.

"So, Mia. Mia Rose Colter. Stealing from your employer."

"No, I didn't."

The detective studied her tear stained face, "That's what you're being charged with, I wasn't asking if you did it."

"I'm telling you I didn't do it."

The overweight male detective flopped in a chair and ignored Mia. He belched, groaned and rubbed his chest.

"Let's not get takeaways from Phin Lee's again."

A knock on the door cut off the woman's reply, she rose and pulled it open; her colleague disregarded Mia and squirmed uncomfortably—his attention turned inward as he struggled with indigestion. Mia ignored the gurgles from his stomach and tried to listen to the hushed conversation at the door. Presently the woman turned back from the door and set a sheet of paper on the desk; she glanced at her colleague and shook her head.

"Well," she said to Mia, "you're free to go."

"What?"

"The person who pointed the finger at you has confessed to planting the money in your bag. So, come with me and I'll get you out of here. Cam, go and take a Quick-eze and pull yourself together."

Cam responded with a muffled burp.

When Mia emerged into the foyer, Raffi jumped to his feet and hurried to her.

"Mia," he hugged her to him, "are you okay?"

"Yes. No."

"They released you didn't they? Without charge I hope."

"Yeah, Kate set me up."

"Yes, I know."

"Raffi, I can't do this. Dylan is scary enough but if Kate—I can't deal with it—"

"Mia? What—"

"I really need the job but if I'm going to be caught up in their problems—I just can't deal with it."

"Mia—don't quit on me. I'm here for you. Don't leave—you're doing a great job, you have a promising future."

"I've never thought I'd ever be arrested—I've never been so frightened!"

"Mia, listen to me. I'll talk to Kate, I'll make her realise the harm she did. She and Dylan better get their act together soon or I'll cut both of them loose." He rubbed her back. "Please, Mia. Don't run away on me."

"I don't—no I want to stay."

Raffi pressed his lips to her forehead. "Come on, I'll get you home." With his arm around her, he guided her through the doors.

"Excuse me!" A man in a grey suit hurried from inside the station, "Wait, can I have a moment?"

"They released her without charge, mate—"

"Yes, I know." The man puffed to a halt. "Mia Colter?"

"Yes."

"Are you Julie Colter's granddaughter?"

"Yes I am."

The man exhaled and smiled.

"I've finally found you. I'm Lloyd Beaufort, Julie's brother."

Mia stared; his words floated around without meaning for a moment and then fell into place; absorbed but not making sense.

"My grandmother didn't have a brother; she said she had no family. She said—"

"I'm sorry to drop this on you after the ordeal you've had this evening; I know you think you have no family—but you do. Julie left home at sixteen and we never saw her again. She and our mother didn't get along. When we found out she had passed away, we visited her grave; the card you left on the flowers was how we knew you even existed."

"Was it you who put the headstone on her grave?"

"Yes, my father—your great-grandfather organised it. He really wants to meet you, Mia. He was heartbroken when my sister left home, nothing would make him happier than to meet you."

Mia's lips trembled and tears blurred her vision. She could see Lloyd's likeness to her grandmother. A little taller than Mia; he had short light brown hair. Her life a series of loved ones dying, she dared not hope she had any relatives left. She didn't remember her mother, and her grandfather died when Mia was too young to remember him. Their loss shadowed her childhood.

"I swear, I'm not some weirdo," said Lloyd. He looked at Raffi. "Are you her boyfriend?"

"Raffi Cheney."

He shook Raffi's hand and Mia noticed Lloyd's eyes widen.

"Raffi—Rafael Cheney?"

"Yes—that's me. Rafael Cheney of El Rodeo fame."

"Sorry, I didn't mean—"

"It's okay," Raffi smiled, "I did the crime and did the time. I learned my lesson and now I'm home earning an honest living."

"I hadn't heard you'd been released."

"I didn't exactly advertise it."

Lloyd's eyes moved back to Mia.

"I'm a lawyer, I follow these things. So, can I get a phone number? I guess you'll want time to think things over, but my father would love to meet you. He's been asking everyday if I've found you."

"Okay." Mia choked back tears; Raffi's arm around her shoulders steadied her. "I'd like to meet him."

"Would lunch tomorrow be okay?"

"Yes." Mia's smile belied her unease; Lloyd seemed pleasant enough, why had her grandmother shut her family out? Should she be wary? Life had taught Mia caution.

"You're welcome to come too." Lloyd turned to Raffi.

Mia's doubt pushed forward.

"Yes, I'll come—that is if Mia wants me along." Raffi looked from Lloyd to Mia.

32

After Lloyd left them, Mia nestled in Raffi's embrace.

"Are you okay, baby?"

She nodded, mute.

"I guess I better get you home. It's been a rough evening for you."

Her arms tightened around him and she shook her head.

"Or you can come home with me."

"I'd like that. I don't want to be alone."

****

Nerves plagued Mia as Raffi opened his front door. She had never been with a man; while her friends strove to lose their virginity Mia stayed home and cared for her grandmother. In spending the night at Raffi's place, she agreed to go to bed with him, didn't she?

Is that what you want, Mia? Of course it is, stupid.

She was nineteen, her friend Ashleigh had lost her virginity four years before.

"Are you sure this is okay?" Raffi's arms settled around her.

"Yes, I'm just nervous."

"I won't bite." His lips brushed her earlobe. "Unless you want me too."

A smile eased the tension on Mia's face; she loved Raffi, the rock she clung to as that day's tide had threatened to wash her away. Lloyd turning up unsettled her, each time she anticipated the next day's meeting with her great-grandfather, a twinge of anxiety roiled in her stomach.

"Now, what am I going to cook for dinner? You must be hungry." Raffi led her into the kitchen.

"Yes, I am."

"Me too. Starving!" He opened the fridge, then in the freezer. "Ah-hah!" He feigned a French accent. "I have one of my mother's seafood Mornay lasagnes."

"Sounds yummy!"

"It is. I hope you're not watching your weight, Mum has been trying to fatten me up since I got back—" His eyelids fluttered and discomfort flickered across his face. He shrugged and grimaced. "Well, I guess you've worked it out by now, I spent two years in jail in Caracas and it wasn't exactly a health farm. Venezuelan prisons are among the worst in the world. Do you drink white wine?"

"Yes."

Raffi removed the dish from the freezer and put it in the oven. Mia watched his long hands set the oven. He took two wine glasses from the cupboard and a bottle of wine from the fridge.

"How did you land in there?"

He grabbed a cheese board and knife and sliced some fruit and cheese; he added a small bowl of crackers and passed it to her.

"Carry that." A smile warmed his black eyes as he picked up the bottle of wine and glasses, "Come and sit down, I'll tell you all about it." Raffi filled their glasses, clinked his against hers, and took a drink, Mia swallowed a sip as he kissed her. "So—when I left school I went to the USA for a gap year..."

Mia listened to his tale. Compared to hers, his life was interesting; at the age of twenty-four, he had clocked up a lot of miles and experience.

"...and I arrived back in Australia feeling pretty battered with more than a few regrets but I learned many things you can't learn at university.

"I got out of that shit-hole three years early, I still don't know why they set me free, but I wasn't going to argue. I have a few theories which I won't scare you with."

"I'm glad you got out when you did. You turned up in my life at the exact right time."

"I'm glad I did too. Girls like you aren't easy to find." His lips found hers—a kiss not of the previous kind, this kiss demanded body and soul. "Two years was a long time to go without sex," he whispered.

"I think I win," Mia said softly, "I haven't been there yet."

"Really? I hope you don't mind me saying it, but you sing the blues like an old slapper."

Mia laughed; her band mates had made similar observations. "Thanks—I think."

Raffi scrutinised her face as though seeing her for the first time. "I'm going to have to take it slow, aren't I?"

Mia remained silent as she watched his eyes, she hoped he wasn't put off by her lack of experience.

"You have pretty eyes—no—pretty everything." His eyelashes tickled her forehead as his lips teased her face, her lips, cheeks, and eyelids. "I don't think I've taken a virgin to my bed before, I'm kind of looking forward to it." He nibbled her ear and kissed her neck, Mia could scarcely breathe.

A ringing sound issued from the kitchen, he sighed and pressed his face into her shoulder.

"There goes the dinner bell," he groaned.

****

Mia had always dreamed the man she'd fall in love with would be like Raffi. He set the table, lit a candle and dimmed the lights. He made her laugh as he told her about his escapades in the USA and South America. He admitted his mistakes and it heartened her when he said he wanted to be good, for her and for his family.

"I've given my parents a lot of grief, but now I'm going to make up for it. I won't rest until I find out what Dylan's problem is. He had everything when I left Australia; he ran the nightclub and made loads of money. He always drank too much, but he had it under control. Now he's destroyed his marriage; he deliberately hurts Kate as if he wants to drive her away. I think he's living at home with his mother some of the time, I don't know where he spends the rest of the time—for all I know he might be homeless."

"I overheard him having an argument with his mother and brother in the loading dock. I didn't mean to eavesdrop, but I was in the dressing room. I just froze and stayed there until they went."

"What were they arguing about?"

"He gave them some photos and told them to keep them—that he didn't care. They seemed anxious about it. It sounded like Dylan knows something about Ollie that could destroy his career."

Raffi frowned and took a sip of his wine. He gazed unseeing at the glass, deep in thought.

Mia set her fork down. "I hope I'm not overstepping the boundaries by telling you about it."

"No, it's okay. I don't know what Dylan would have over Ollie. Who knows, Ollie is a creep—anyway, they're a pretty dysfunctional mob, always were. I think that's why Dad took up with Mum; he made a mistake marrying old Shirley."

"He's still married to her, isn't he?"

"Yeah. He lives with Mum though." Raffi smiled. "Can't say I blame him. Shirley is an old snake, steer well clear of her, Mia."

Mia remembered Shirley referring to Raffi as 'the French whore's bastard.' She didn't mention it to Raffi though she had a feeling he wouldn't care anyway.

Mia helped Raffi stack their plates in the dishwasher and as she dried her hands, Raffi's arms slipped around her from behind. He kissed her neck and his hands explored her body.

"We don't have to do this, if you'd rather wait. If you're not ready—"

"No, I want to. I'm ready."

He took her hand, led her to his bedroom and began to undress her. Shirt first and a kiss—demanding and forceful. He unbuttoned her jeans and pushed them off her hips. He removed his shirt and Mia gasped at the long scar down his ribs, it ran from below his armpit down to his waist.

"War wound," he inhaled at her touch.

"Raffi?"

"I'll tell you about it someday."

He pushed her bra straps off her shoulders, unclasped and flung it aside.

Mia shivered at his light touch on her breasts.

"Nice," he whispered.

He stripped off her knickers, and pushed her to the bed, she fell with a soft bounce and watched him undress.

She trembled a little as he lay down and pulled her against him. He teased her with his hands and mouth, his body warm and hard.

"Raffi…"

"No, not yet. We're going slowly, remember?"

He spread her legs and gently teased her, fingers first, then his tongue, the stubble on his face scuffed the tender skin of her thighs. Mia never knew her body could feel like this; her muscles tensed, a sweet ache deep inside only he could ease. Beside her again, his mouth was on hers, she tasted herself on his lips. She closed her eyes as he parted her legs and slid into her. She whimpered at the twinge of pain. He moved inside her slowly, his breathing came in unsteady puffs as he filled her again and again. Her arms tightened around him as her hips came up to meet him.

"Tell me if I'm hurting."

"No, it's not hurting, not now.

He moved faster, Mia wondered at how her body could feel such sweet torment, it built up and up, an ache needing release—like scratching an itch. She couldn't stop the cry that escaped with the searing peak, wave after aching wave. Raffi moaned as he pushed hard, it hurt but elated her.

"Sorry!" He panted, "I couldn't control myself."

"No—that was—I didn't know it would feel so good."

As they slept, entwined, Mia discovered Raffi didn't sleep well. He frequently thrashed about and startled awake but settled back to sleep at her touch.

In the morning, Mia frowned with embarrassment and apologised for the spot of blood on his sheets.

"Hey, it's okay. We should frame it and hang it on the wall." He pushed her onto her back and licked her nipples. "A memory of our first time together."

"Your mother might find that a little tacky."

He laughed, "Hm, I dunno about that, I moved into this unit to get away from listening to her and Dad going at it in the middle of the night. I've always heard women in their forties are horny and now I believe it."

33

Jim Beaufort took his seat at the corner table and watched as Lloyd sat opposite. Jim's nervousness at meeting his great-granddaughter was out of character in this worldly man. His daughter, Julie had the same nature as her mother, head strong and volatile. By the time she left, the two women could not be in the same room without snarling at each other. He hoped Mia was more even tempered.

"Dad, I have to warn you, Mia's boyfriend is that younger step-brother of Oliver Jackson's. Rafael Cheney, you remember, the one they sent to prison in Venezuela? He seems pleasant enough; I just thought I should give you fair warning."

Before Jim had time to think on it, Lloyd got to his feet.

"Here they are."

Jim had somehow expected Mia to be petite and fair-haired like Julie. The girl moving nervously towards them was darkhaired, taller than average and slim. The tall thin man who held her hand, Jim vaguely recognised from the news reports a few years before.

"Mia," Lloyd kissed the girl's cheek, "I'm glad you could make it. Raffi…" He shook hands with her companion. "Dad, this is your great-granddaughter."

She hesitated before stepping into his arms.

"Mia," he said, "I'm so happy we found you. I'm sorry you lost your grandmother; I wish I could have seen her again."

The girl cried, and he held her, tears welled in Jim's eyes.

"I didn't know I had any family left," she whispered.

When they left the restaurant a couple of hours later, Jim was the happiest he'd been in years. His great-granddaughter was intelligent and amiable. She promised to visit him on the next Saturday. Hurt at the loss of his daughter all those years before lessened, finding this beautiful young woman had healed some of the hurt.

34

Home from her gig, in the early hours of the morning, Mia sifted through her grandmother's possessions. She found they contained family photos and albums, jewellery, mementos, and ornaments. Her grandmother's birth certificate was the only thing to confirm Jim Beaufort's existence. In a long, flat box, she found Lilly's things. Mia fanned the pages of one of her journals; seven of them, full of her aunt's childish handwriting. Lily was a mixture of child and woman; a prolific artist and writer. On the few occasions Mia had heard her speak, Lily was quite articulate. At the bottom of the small pile of stationary lay a thick A3 sketchbook with hundreds of pencil sketches—mostly faces—and mostly those of her family. Mia recognised her own face among them, from her babyhood until age thirteen. Then Lily died. Happy faces and sad—

sometimes afraid. The drawings that intrigued her most—that Mia knew from family photos—were of her mother. Completed in minute detail, Lily would rub out some features. Usually the eyes and occasionally the mouth. A drawing of Rosie's shaved head bore a long scar across the back. The most poignant were drawings of her mother lying on a bed, wasted limbs contorted, her stomach distended with pregnancy—and some depicted her connected to a life-support machine. Her aunt's attention to detail amazed Mia. Lily's artistry developed; her skill had increased with each year of her brief life. Evidence of frustration etched across some pages; angry scribbles uncharacteristic of the sensitive artistry elsewhere. Many sketches depicted the faces of two young men and every few pages she had sketched a hand with an S and the word 'Dal' across the back, sometimes the word was 'Del.' On some pages, she had crossed out the S. Occasionally, two circles lay inside the loops of the S. In one sketch, the hand held a rock of indeterminate size. The hand encompassed the rock, which faded into white paper. The last drawing was of Lilly herself, her eyes wide, her hands over her ears and her mouth contorted in a scream, a deluge of tears flowed down her face—or was it blood? Beside the drawing, the same hand, this time with a symbol Mia knew well. The squashed S with a slash and two dots, underneath, the words *Dal Segno*—a music symbol and the words translated, meant 'by sign.'

Mia gasped and jumped to her feet; under the hand, her aunt had sketched the familiar ending to a stanza of music with the sign and the words, *'Dal Segno'* instructed the performer to go back and repeat from the symbol. The closing stanza of the piece Mia had performed for her grade five piano exam. Her aunt's photographic memory astounded Mia. She remembered Lily running, screaming from the room.

"Is that what upset you, Lily?" she whispered.

Mia gathered Lily's journals and sat on the bed; she read them in order, from beginning to end. The sky outside her window had turned pink as the last piece dropped into place. Her pain and tears increased with the early morning birdsong. In her child-like way, Lily had revealed all Mia wondered about herself. She wiped the tears from her face as she turned the last page. Now she understood how she came to be, and why her grandmother would never speak of it. It wasn't embarrassment at an unwanted teenage pregnancy that had silenced her grandmother; it was horror. Had Lily been right when, as an eight-year old, she wrote in her large, childish hand? *'Daddy died today, he jumped off The Gap because the policeman said he could not help us anymore. It's my fault. Why can't I tell the policeman what happened? I don't know how to tell them. I just can't make the words come out.'*

Mia realized why the space on her birth certificate that should carry the name of her father said, 'Unknown.' Her father was one of her mother's rapists; one of those who had bludgeoned Rosie Colter with a rock and left her for dead, brain damaged, blind, and pregnant.

Why didn't Nanna tell me? She knew I would read Lily's diary and find out—or could Nanna have chosen not to read them herself?

Mia had read when a mother died, the daughter's mourning would never end. Mia had never had a mother, only a flesh and blood vessel to grow her until viable. Even if she could have spoken to her mother at birth, her mother couldn't speak back. Mia was born to a mother gone from the living world.

For the first time in her life, she allowed herself self-pity. Lily's legacy left her with a mountain to climb. She hugged herself and sobbed. It went through her mind to call Ashleigh, her friend's irritation if woken at that early hour would be duly noted. Ashleigh was a fair-weather friend.

She turned thoughts to Raffi and her newly found relatives, Lloyd and Jim. Her mind circled back to the horror that had brought her into the world. An innocent baby conceived of a vicious crime. She didn't know where the crime had taken place; the rapists remained at large. Lily, at the age of five, had witnessed the horror in its entirety and it destroyed her young mind. Her mother, Rosie was just fourteen years old when she gave birth to Mia via caesarean section. Then the doctors turned off the machines that kept her alive for the last two months of Mia's gestation. It rebounded, time and again. One of those rapists had fathered her. *My father is a criminal.* Each time the thought renewed itself, a sick swooping sensation churned her stomach. They had destroyed her mother's life; the violence that gave life to Mia had devastated the Colter family.

I'm a freak! My conception was a crime! Mia roamed the streets, oblivious to the city around her, her mind fixed inward. She found herself on a bus to Blacktown. The aches in her muscles unheeded as she stumbled along the gravel path—past the warbling magpie to the graves of her family. Her mother's headstone cooled her cheek as Mia's tears fell.

"I'm so sorry, Rosie. I'm so sorry."

As her sobs faded to exhaustion, the need to share her pain crystalized. She recalled her early teens, lying in the dark revealing her deepest secrets to Ashleigh. She rose from the grave and took out her phone. A minute into her confession, Mia cursed herself—Ashleigh was a different person to the one she had poured her innermost secrets to as a thirteen year old.

"Ew! That's disgusting!"

"Oh, fuck off, Ashleigh—you're disgusting!" Mia hung up. "Fuck you, Ashleigh!" The magpie's warbles fell silent; the bird tipped his head and listened to Mia's tirade. "Fuck your fat arse all the way to Bullamakanka! I hope you choke! Fuck you and the horse you squashed into the ground when you rode in on it! Fuck you!"

Anger scorched as Mia sprinted to the bus stop. Ashleigh's response had upset her beyond repair and burned that last bridge to her high school friends. She had postponed it too long. She panted to a halt at the bus stop and took out her phone. Puffing from her exertions, she called Christopher and told him she didn't want to see him anymore.

"It's that gangster boss of yours isn't it?"

Mia laughed. "Yes, Christopher, as a matter of fact it is." She hung up before he could reply. Cruel—but she would not listen to his recriminations. Instead, she focused on the future. The tragic circumstances of her conception troubled Mia, yet she thanked those who had allowed her birth. Though tragedy and heartache dominated her childhood, she was a healthy, well-educated young woman, and in spite of her underprivileged upbringing, an above average musician. She had a natural talent for singing and performing—and she had Raffi. Mia smiled and a tear fell on her cheek.

That night her band and many in the audience listened in awe as Mia sang the blues with renewed passion.

"Jesus, Mia!" Luke patted her shoulder with a shaking hand. "I think you're channelling Bessie Smith herself!"

35

Raffi had just thanked his mother for helping him clean the club and saw her out the back door when Dylan appeared.

"Raffi! You sneaky cunt, you're always telling me to stay out of the bar, now I've caught you, red-handed."

"Come and have a coffee with me, Dylan. I want to talk to you."

"I'll only talk if it's an Irish coffee, Bro."

Raffi looked at his watch and sighed; midday approached. "Okay, Irish coffee then." Raffi went about making coffee and Dylan slouched in the chair beside Raffi's desk.

"Where's Kate today?" Dylan gazed around the door into Kate's empty office.

Raffi glanced up from adding whiskey; his stepbrother's indigo eyes caught his attention. He'd seen eyes like that somewhere else…

"I gave her a week off. That's what I want to talk to you about."

Dylan frowned. "What's up with her, is she sick?"

Raffi set the cup on the desk beside Dylan and sat down.

"Nothing a bit of love and affection from you wouldn't fix."

"She threw me out, what can I do about it?"

"You could start by keeping your dick in your pants."

"What and deprive all those women out there of my sterling service?"

"I'm serious, Dylan. The night before last, they took Mia to the police station, accused her of stealing money out of my safe."

"What? I thought she was your girlfriend."

"She is my girlfriend. But Kate thought she was your girlfriend, and she decided she'd take action to get rid of her."

"Ah, Kate gets jealous…"

"Because you torment her with your womanising!"

"Gotta show her what she's missing—"

"Bullshit! She knows what she's missing. Why the fuck do you have to keep hurting her?"

Dylan didn't answer; he took a long swig from his coffee.

"Dylan, what is it? What's eating you? Why are you so hell-bent on destroying yourself and the woman you love most?"

Dylan looked up at him; distress flashed in his eyes.

"If you're depressed you can get help, you know. Or you can talk to me, I won't tell anyone else."

"If I told you what my problem is, Bro, I'd have to kill you."

"Dylan, I'm serious!"

"So am I, Raff." He got to his feet, drained his cup and belched. "You and Pat are worth ten of Ollie and Shirley, you know that?"

Where did that come from?

"Dylan, you've got to get it together. Please?"

"I like to oblige you little brother but me and together are never gonna be."

"Dylan, I want you to come back here and work."

His stepbrother laughed.

"I mean it, when you're on your game you're a good people person and I need a new bar manager."

"Why?"

"Because Frankie is organising the restaurant."

"Why don't you get Grennie to do it?"

"I don't trust Grennie if you must know."

"Why?"

"Instinct." *His eyes are too close together.* "I want you as my bar manager."

"Why?"

"Because I know you're the best fucking barman in Sydney. The job is yours, Dylan. Please?"

"That would be like putting Ossie Osborne in charge of the bat cave."

Raffi laughed. "Oh, fuck off." He watched Dylan move to the door. "But think about it, and for Christ's sake, I'm serious—go talk to your wife. Work something out!"

"I'll think about it over a drink or two."

"I dare say you will."

36

Kate had woken early, she had a lot of catching up to do at work; taking a week off hadn't solved anything. She hadn't seen Dylan and had spent most of the time feeling ill and so tired, she only wanted to sleep. She picked her outfit from her wardrobe and went to take a shower, but she had a small task to take care of before anything else. Couple of minutes later, the double blue lines on the pregnancy test kit brought bile to her throat. She had stopped taking the pill after she threw Dylan out, she'd had no intentions of getting involved with anyone else, and she didn't expect he'd come back wanting her again. She should have known she was ovulating, given how horny she had felt. Now here she was at age thirty-four, single and pregnant. Her chances of getting back together with Dylan seemed negligent.

At twenty-seven, Kate landed the job at Dylan's Blues Club. When Dylan interviewed her, she fell under his spell. When he discovered she had trained as a hairdresser he demanded a haircut. She cut his hair shaved his face. By the time she had finished, they'd fallen in love; he spent every night at her house and made her his wife several months later.

Now what am I going to do?

She showered and wrapped herself in her bathrobe, moving automatically, her mind fixed on her dilemma. As she finished applying her makeup, she stared at her pale face and could scarcely believe her situation. Tyres crunched the gravel on the driveway below and a car door closed. Dylan half fell from a taxi. She could pretend she wasn't home but her car parked in the drive gave her away. Instead, she let him in.

He closed the door behind him and leaned on it, swaying. He hadn't shaved or showered in twenty-four hours and smelled like a distillery. Lately, every time she saw him, he looked angry.

"Dylan, I need to talk to you."

"Talk? Fuck that, you smell nice, come here!"

He dragged her into a clumsy embrace, his mouth crushed hers; his hands bruised where he grabbed handfuls of flesh. She gave a startled cry as he picked her up and carried her to the lounge.

"Dylan, no!"

"Yes!" he growled and pushed her bathrobe open. "Yes!"

"I said no, Dylan!"

He spread her legs and began licking and biting her.

"You're the sexiest woman I know." He kissed her thigh.

"Dylan, please listen." Kate pulled away, rolled off the couch and tried to stand; he pulled her face down on the carpet.

It hurt as he grabbed her hips and lifted her.

"You want it, you always want it."

He fumbled, warm against her thigh then forced his way inside her.

"Dylan! No!"

"Yes!"

"You're hurting me!"

It surprised her when he stopped and got to his feet; he held out a hand and pulled her up. He carried her to the bedroom and laid her on the bed. He pulled off his clothes and moved over her. He kissed her tenderly and held her close. Once again on top of her, this time he made love to her the way he used to.

"You like it like that don't you?"

"Yes, I do," she whispered.

"You like it rough too…"

"No, Dylan, not today."

"Why not? You always cum when I go hard," he growled and pushed. "You love it—you love me, don't you?"

"You know I do. I just want you to be the man I married."

"He drowned." He kissed her neck. "In a sea of alcohol."

"No, Dylan."

Suddenly he stopped and rolled off her. "Can you keep a secret?"

"Of course."

"I mean a deadly secret, one that could get both of us killed."

"Dylan?"

"I'm serious, Kate. You can't repeat this, not for my sake, for yours."

"Then why tell me?"

"Soon I won't be able to drink enough to drown it. I have to tell someone or I'm going to go mad."

"You can trust me, Dylan," Kate propped herself on one elbow to watched his face.

"When I was fourteen, I raped a girl."

"Raped?" Kate didn't know what to say. Dylan often flirted aggressively and enjoyed rough sex but he had a gentle soul. "Boys do stupid things—"

"I was fourteen, but Ollie was eighteen and he dragged the girl into the bushes and raped her. When he finished, he pushed me, he told me to stop being a poof—you know, be a man—and I was just a stupid kid and got all caught up in the lust. Watching him go at it made me horny. I was as bad as him by the time I finished." He swallowed and sniffled.

"Ollie scares me. I don't know—there's something about him."

"Keep being scared of him. He's a head case. He bashed the girl with a rock and left her brain damaged. She died less than a year later."

Kate gasped.

"Did you face charges?"

"No, we were down the coast on holidays and old Shirley got Ollie out of there in the middle of the night, one of her dodgy, gangster friends picked him up in a boat and got him back home. She brought me home two days later. The police stopped our car but I was a baby-faced fourteen-year old. They were searching for two men, one with some kind of tattoo on his hand, apparently the girls little sister witnessed the whole thing. I was tall so the little girl probably saw me as a man, not a spotty fourteen year old. Ollie had some stupid tattoo on the back of his hand from when he tried to learn guitar—he thought he'd become a rock star in three easy lessons—dickhead. Mum got a crooked tattoo artist to remove the tatt with some dodgy laser equipment—she could hardly take him to a doctor given all the publicity." Tears leaked from his eyes.

"We got away with it. Ollie was the Sand Dune Killer, I don't know if you remember all that from back then. He'd raped them and then bash their head in so they wouldn't talk. I had a sick hero-worship of my big brother; I used to follow him around. He goaded me into becoming as bad as him. It would never have occurred to me to drag that girl off into the bushes and rape her. She was only thirteen. Once I had helped Ollie rape her, he had me where he wanted me, if I went to the police I would be dobbing myself in. I was scared shitless."

Dylan sniffed and puffed out a breath, his forearm lay across his eyes.

Kate moved closer.

"You want to know why I crawl into the bottle, Kate. Now you know."

Kate drew an arm over him. "I love you, Dylan, no matter what; I love you. What are you going to do?"

"I don't know. Give me time to think about it. If I go to the police, I doubt I would be the only one in danger. You will be. Ollie and Shirley know I'm very fond of Raffi and his little brothers; they would be in danger too. I might be sent to prison."

"You were only fourteen when you committed the crime—"

"Yeah, but I've kept silent for twenty years, I would probably do time."

"Maybe not if you plea bargain."

"That's an option. If I go to the police, the safest place for me is in prison, but if I'm in prison, what happens to you? And Raffi, Nic, and little Patrick?"

"Do you really think they'd come after us?"

"I wouldn't put anything past my mother and brother. Mum enjoys the prestige of having a politician son; can you imagine the scandal if he's proven to be a serial killer and rapist? And Mum knew about it so she is just as guilty."

"You could deny you raped the girl too—"

"No." Dylan laughed cynically, "no can do."

"Why not? You've kind of lied all these years by keeping silent, so why not—"

"DNA. They still have the DNA taken from the girl and though they never said it at the time, I'll bet the police knew the rapists were brothers. Or at least, half-brothers."

He sat up, plumped the pillows and leaned back against the bed head.

"Anyway, what did you want to talk to me about?"

"Oh—um, it doesn't matter."

"No, come on. You were going to ask for a divorce, weren't you?"

"No."

"Well, then what?"

"I'm pregnant."

"Tell me you're joking."

37

At the top of Raffi's House of Blues, a room made by building a floor into the old fly loft, stored all the old furniture. Mia and Raffi sorted through years of discarded chairs, tables, and boxes of junk. As they worked they tossed about names with no serious contenders. Raffi's Roost an almost and the Horney Hamster had them both in stitches.

"Are you sure you don't mind helping us with this?" She smiled at Raffi's grimy face.

"Of course I don't mind."

"I want to get all the dirty work done before the restaurant below opens." He wrapped his arms around her and gave her a resounding kiss. The building work complete on the restaurant below, it just needed the finishing touches.

"I love helping you; it gives me an excuse to spend the day with you." She tried to wipe a spot of dust off his nose but added more.

"It's not the healthiest place to be."

"Well, we're nearly done; I've just got one more drawer to go through in that filing cabinet and then we can start vacuuming."

"I'm getting specialist cleaners in to do that."

"Spoil-sport."

The drawer of the old filing cabinet squeaked with years of disuse as Mia pulled it open. "Looks like more of Dylan's book keeping—" She stopped and lifted out a framed photo and blew the dust off it. "Who's this?"

Raffi didn't hear her as he dragged a stack of old chairs across the wooden floor. Mia studied the photo of two young men, their faces smiled up at her. She recognised Dylan; he looked about thirteen.

"Who's this with Dylan?" she repeated when Raffi stopped his racket. He stepped over to look at the photo.

"Ollie. Dylan would have put it up here so he didn't have to look at Ollie's sour face."

"Is Ollie really that bad?"

Raffi grinned and returned to the stack of chairs, "I wouldn't piss on him if he was on fire."

Mia could see what he meant about the sour face; Ollie wasn't half as handsome as his younger brother. He had twisted, irregular features and his thin, cruel mouth evident even as he had smiled for the camera. She wiped the dust from the glass and froze. Over Dylan's shoulder draped the hand from Lily's drawings. Even upside down, she recognised the words 'Dal Segno.' The symbol like a squashed S with a line and two dots. Mia's stomach churned, her heart raced. Could this be them? The men who had raped her mother? If so, then one of them was her father.

She looked around to see where Raffi forced chairs into the dumbwaiter. She slipped the photo from its frame, folded and stuffed it into the pocket of her jacket.

****

Dust and cobwebs coated the old furniture from upstairs. Raffi ordered Mia to stand back while he, Pat, and Dylan loaded them into the removalist's van. By the time they finished, all three men sneezed and cursed. Mia watched Dylan blow his nose on a tissue, toss it at the bin and miss. When all three men went out into the laneway, discussing their next move; Mia gritted her teeth, grabbed a wad of tissues and picked up the one Dylan had discarded. She wrapped it carefully and stashed it in her backpack. Her face burned, the security cameras would have recorded her actions. She hoped Raffi would have no reason to check the stored footage.

Later that afternoon, Mia made her way into the city to meet Lloyd and Jim for coffee. She had met them only weeks ago and they played an important part in her life.

After they'd finished their coffee, Mia steeled herself. She hoped Lloyd wouldn't think her odd or tasteless with such a request.

"Lloyd, I wonder if you could help me with something."

"Sure, if it's humanly possible."

Mia pulled out the wad of tissues she had stored in a small plastic bag. "There's a snotty tissue in here."

"Ew!"

"I'm sorry, I don't normally go around collecting discarded tissues but this is important. I wonder if you could tell me where I can have it tested for DNA—and mine—I want to compare them. I want to find out if the DNA on this tissue is related to me."

"Mia? Who—"

"I want to know if he's my father, or uncle—or not related at all."

Lloyd's face held a hundred questions and Mia appreciated his tact.

"Okay. Give it to me, I'll also need a blood sample of yours—do you have a pin or something? We'll need a daub of blood on a piece of paper. I'll get it done. These tests aren't always accurate, you know."

Mia bit her lip and nodded. This could open a can of worms for herself and Raffi's family. The issue had plagued her all morning; she had to know.

"How long does it take?"

"About a week I think."

When Mia kissed Lloyd and Jim goodbye and dream walked to the bus, she worried she sailed into a storm. She recoiled at the notion she might prove herself the daughter of Oliver Jackson MP. She instinctively disliked the man. Raffi hated him and his mother—what if their blood flowed in her veins? What traits might have hitched a ride with their DNA? This revelation she sought could come at a terrible cost.

****

On tenterhooks over the coming week, Mia paced like a caged animal; other times she sat, paralysed. She regretted her haste and failed to stem the frustrated tears. She did and didn't want a positive result. She didn't know what she would do—did she go to the police? She worried she would destroy her relationship with Raffi who meant more to her than anyone. Was it worth it? Did it matter? Each time she went through it in her head she came to the same conclusion—she had to know who her father was. Her world now in painful awry instead of the blissful ignorance she had lived until Lily's dead ink had turned dal segno to mean more than 'by sign.'

Each night, as she entertained the crowds in Raffi's House of Blues, she watched Dylan mingle with the patrons.

Could he be my father?

If it came to a choice, he'd be better than his brother. His brown hair the same shade as hers, his eyes the same blue. Could he be a rapist? He seemed just a harmless, knock-about drunk. People liked him; he had an easy charm.

The days dragged on and two weeks later Lloyd arrived early morning at her doorstep. She let him into her shabby living room, numbness awaited.

"Mia, sit down, I've got that result."

Mia quailed and nodded.

"That man, the DNA—he is your father."

"Oh, god—" Mia gave way to a flood of tears.

"Is that not a good thing?"

"No—it's not. Well maybe—oh god!"

"Mia—"

"Can you let me think it over? Please?"

"Mia, I don't want to leave you alone when you're so upset."

"Please Lloyd, I'm okay. I'm not going to do anything stupid. I just need to get my head around it—work out what to do."

"Well, if you're sure."

"I'll tell you about it. Soon. I just need to think."

"Well, I'll be in court all day but text me if you want to talk, it might take a few hours for me to answer but I promise I will."

Mia always imagined if she found her father, he would be older, around fifty with greying hair, like the fathers of her school friends. Which, she figured, was stupid given her mother gave birth at age fourteen. She had at first feared Dylan, then she'd come to realise he existed a sad figure—a damaged man. She instinctively wanted to run but she couldn't bear to lose Raffi. Step one was to tell Raffi, Lloyd, and Jim her secret; step two—well she'd deal with step one first.

38

Mia carried the flat box that contained Lily's sketchbook and diaries into Raffi's unit. She shut the door and kissed Raffi. He followed her into the sitting room. Jim and Lloyd had arrived before her, Lloyd had a glass of scotch and Jim drank beer from a clear glass bottle.

"Now my mysterious Mia, before you put us out of our misery, can I get you a drink?"

"Yes, something strong."

"I have Scotch."

"That would be perfect." She tried to smile but worried she may have grimaced.

He returned and set the drink down on the coffee table and sat beside her.

"Now," said Lloyd, "what is this all about?"

Jim sat forward and rested his elbows on his knees.

"It's about my mother—" Mia choked back a sob.

Don't start crying already!

"My mother and how I came to be."

Raffi took her hand. "It's okay, take your time."

"My mother was thirteen years old when she was raped by two men."

Lloyd jumped to his feet. "Shit! The Rosie Colter case—why didn't I make the connection?" He turned back to Mia, "but how does this—"

"She became pregnant to one of the rapists—with me."

Jim moved to sit on her other side and patted her shoulder.

"And you know who he is." Lloyd stared. "How—it's a cold case—how did you work it out?"

"If you're familiar with the case, you'll remember Rosie's little sister witnessed the whole thing, apparently all she could tell the police was—"

"That it was two men and one had a tattoo on his hand."

"It destroyed her but she left me with enough drawings and journal entries to work it out. Lily was an amazing artist."

Mia opened Lily's sketchbook and showed them the last pages first. She told them about Lily running screaming from the room when she saw the dal segno sign on her music sheet.

"Holy shit! Look at this!"

"But we don't know who this guy is." Raffi looked from Mia to Lloyd, then at the page of the sketchbook.

Mia reached into her backpack and pulled out the photo of Dylan and Ollie. Her lip trembled as she handed it to him.

"Dylan's my father," she whispered.

"What? How—"

"We've done a DNA test, Raffi." Lloyd sat down, his eyes on Raffi.

"Really? Jesus!" Raffi studied the photo. Mia watched a wave of confusion battle with disbelief across his face.

Mia told them about how she overheard the conversation between Dylan, Shirley, and Ollie. How she'd found the photo upstairs and kept it. About the discarded tissue.

"There's one major snag here," Lloyd studied the drawing then the photo of Dylan and Ollie, "We collected that DNA sample illegally. It won't stand up in court. I doubt Lily's drawings and diaries would either."

"I might have to have a talk to Dylan, what year did this happen?"

"1994." Mia and Lloyd spoke in unison.

"Dylan would have been a minor; about…" Raffi went quiet, counting on his fingers. "He would have been about fourteen and that would have made Ollie at least eighteen."

"An adult."

"This is Oliver Jackson, the politician we're talking about, isn't it?" Jim spoke for the first time.

"Yes. Fucking creep!"

"You and I share the same sentiments about Mr Jackson it would seem." Lloyd smiled.

"I hate him and that old dragon he calls his mother."

"The only way we can be sure to bring him to justice is if Dylan turns states evidence. What kind of person is Dylan?"

"He's the only decent member of that family—he'd be a nice bloke if he wasn't such a hopeless alcoholic. If he didn't drink he'd be a successful man. He's having problems with his marriage at the moment, nothing he couldn't fix by knocking off the booze and women."

"I think Shirley might have known about it."

Mia recounted Shirley's word to her sons, *'I fixed it for you, don't fuck it up.'*

****

Raffi leaned on the bar watching the crowd, all eyes fixed on Mia as she sang 'Blackest Day.' He smiled, for one so young she sang the blues like a jaded old diva.

"She's really something, isn't she?"

Raffi looked around; Dylan stood beside him.

"Dylan, just the man I need to see."

"Is it about the bar manager's job? I dunno Raffi; you could do a lot better than employing me."

Raffi turned to the bar and gestured to one of the barkeeps.

"A scotch for me and a rum for Dylan, please, Tim."

The barman got the drinks and set them on the counter.

"Get your drink and come with me."

Dylan followed as Raffi weaved through the crowd of people, up the stairs to the foyer and through the door that opened into the corridor to Raffi's office.

"Now, there's something I need to discuss with you, Dylan."

"I've talked to Kate. She and I are giving it another go."

"Good."

"But that's not what this is about, is it?"

"No." Raffi rubbed his face and leaned back. He picked up his glass then set it back down. "Dylan, I've found out something—something that involves you. Ollie too."

He watched his stepbrother turn pale and gulp a mouthful of his drink and cough.

"You have?"

"The thing you wouldn't tell me because you'd have to kill me."

His stepbrother froze, his eyes fixed on Raffi.

"The Rosie Colter case."

Dylan sat his drink on the desk with a shaking hand, his face turned pale. He shook his head, "How did—"

"Mia is Rosie Colter's daughter."

Dylan scrutinized Raffi closely, taking in his face inch by inch. Raffi watched him process the information.

"But—but she died; I remember the news, months later."

"Nine months later to be exact. The baby was born by caesarean section and the doctors turned off the machines that kept Rosie alive."

Raffi watched the expression in Dylan's eyes change; he watched his words hit home as his brother's eyelids fluttered. He didn't speak.

"Mia was that baby. She's your daughter."

"Bullshit," Dylan whispered. "No—"

"She collected some DNA from you and had it tested."

"She—You let her do that?"

Raffi flicked his hand, palm up. "No, I had no hand in it. Mia found the photo, the one you stored in the old filing cabinet upstairs. She recognised the tattoo on Ollie's hand from those her aunt had drawn. Her aunt was the little girl who witnessed the crime. There is no doubt, they double checked."

Dylan picked at the fabric on the armrest of his chair. Raffi waited, he gave his stepbrother time to take it in. He watched as Dylan puffed out a breath and smacked the armrest with the heel of his hand.

"Christ!" He got to his feet and moved to the window. "Gotta—I've gotta turn myself in, haven't I?"

"Mia's uncle is a lawyer; he said you could probably get immunity if you turn states evidence. You were a minor. Which one of you—"

"Ollie. Which one of us hit her with the rock? Ollie. Fucking mad bastard. The thing is, is Ollie can't know about this—he'll either put out a hit on all of us or he'll flee the country. Mia's mother isn't the only girl he killed. I remember them saying they had matched the DNA to other rapes, other assaults and murders—they know there is a connection."

"You mean you knew about—"

"I was a skinny kid; he used to beat the shit out of me. I hero-worshipped the bastard and followed him everywhere. That's how I knew what he was. He knew I knew and he tricked me into being there when he grabbed Rosie Colter…"

Raffi listened with dull horror as Dylan related the event that gave Mia life.

Dylan sat down, elbows on his knees and covered his face; motionless and quiet. "Of course I would be the father." He waved a shaking hand beside his head. "Ollie had a bout of the mumps when he was fifteen. He's infertile. That's why he doesn't have any kids."

Minutes ticked by and neither man spoke. The room silent save a fan oscillating above; the muffled beat of Mia and the Modes resonated through the building. Dylan sniffed and drained his glass. "I wish I could be proud to be Mia's father."

"One day—"

Dylan rose so fast he startled Raffi.

"Well, there's only one thing to do. Go and hand myself in."

"No, wait! I'll call Lloyd and get him to recommend a good lawyer. Please, Dylan, wait. If you just go in and make a confession you might make things a lot worse for yourself."

"Okay, where do I sign up?"

39

The wind lifted Oliver Jackson's brown hair to a receding hairline. He fumbled with the scissors his assistant had handed him and took his position on the makeshift podium. A public appearance in his position as a minister of the state often made his testicles tingle and he would smile a secret smile. Only he knew his secret smile—the left corner of his mouth turned down, the right curled up and his lips formed a thin curved line.

Power!

When his power sneaked up on him in an unguarded moment, it gave him a rush, a spine-tingling glow that as a young man called Blitz, he'd only achieved by deadly force.

Power!

The group of dignitaries took their seats, his beautiful wife and his mother, both paragons of sophisticated modern womanhood sat at the edge of the audience. He loved these events, the media crowded around chatting and joking among themselves.

But not today.

Today the appearance of his wayward brother pricked the swelling bubble of Oliver's self-importance. Today had held the promise of another successful event until Dylan arrived, handsome and respectable in his best suit; the ever-present cloud of alcohol fumes rippled the air around him.

The host finished her welcome speech and began her preamble to inviting Oliver Jackson MP to open the Martina Roth Women's Crisis Shelter. Oliver tried to catch his mother's eye, to warn her Dylan stood at the back of the gathering. Too late the crowd burst into applause, Oliver marshalled his dignified face and stepped up to the lectern.

"Good morning." He pitched his voice down to a well-practiced orotund quality. "My fellow citizens, thank you for being here today. I am honoured to have the privilege of opening the Martina Roth Women's Crisis Shelter."

Oliver took a breath; he cast a quick glance at where he'd last sighted his brother. His stomach clenched, he wasn't there.

Where is he?

"In today's world, gender stereotypes and sexism are everywhere. The rape culture we thought was in the past is still far too common and violence against women is not receiving anywhere near the attention it should. At least one woman dies a week as a result of domestic violence. To me, the fact that one in four women has experienced sexual harassment at some point in their life is disturbing to say the least. Gender disparity—"

Oliver's narration faltered as someone blew their nose with a trumpet blast; his eyes fell on Dylan who stood at the opposite side of the crowd to Shirley. He wiped his nose, grinned and gave Oliver the thumbs up.

"Our focus must be more on teaching our sons and brothers the right behaviour…"

Dylan sneezed, coughed and cleared his throat. A few well-to-do guests looked around, scandalised. Oliver caught sight of his mother hurrying around the back of the crowd, her eyes fixed on her youngest son.

"Schools must discuss topics such as consensual sex, sexism, and gender equality…"

Whispering drifted to Oliver's ears and he couldn't stop himself from glancing at his mother and brother.

"Shh! Ma, Ollie's speaking!" Dylan remonstrated his mother.

Oliver had prepared a ten-minute speech but opted to cut it short.

"And so it is with great pleasure I declare the Martina Roth Rape Centre open."

He opened his mouth to correct his blunder then shut it again. The audience applauded as he reached over and snipped the cord. A brass plaque shone golden against the black marble monument in the white pebble-garden. He hoped nobody noticed he had called the new women's shelter a rape centre. The title an in-joke among the parliamentary boys-club.

40

A blast of humid air greeted Frankie Cheney as he arrived at the Galeão International Airport in Rio de Janeiro at midday. Sherrie and the kids lingered on his mind as he negotiated customs and immigration. He had one small bag; the company would supply his clothing and everything else. Northern Brazil Security welcomed one of their best men back, if only for a week. His former boss, Jaco Vega greeted him as he emerged and retrieved his bag off the carousel.

"Frankie! Good to see you, amigo!" Jaco greeted Frankie with a muscular hug and shook his hand.

"Good to see you too, Jaco. How is business?"

"Same as always. Our friends up north keep us busy. We would like you back with us, Frankie."

"One week is all I can spare, Jaco. I have a restaurant to run back in Sydney."

"Ah yes! Your other work—I forget you are not always a mercenary."

"No—not anymore—but this time it's personal, Jaco."

"Where did you get this intelligence?"

"Let's discuss it somewhere less public."

"Yes, of course."

"How many men do we have?"

"I can spare forty."

"Should be enough. Do many of them speak English?"

"Not all, sorry, but one is good at rapid translation, I'll put him on your team."

"Thank you. That'll work well for me."

"The DEA are going to richly reward us!" Jaco held up his hand and rubbed his fingertips across his thumb-pad.

"Give the boys a bonus—I just want him shut down for good."

****

Frankie had remained motionless for hours; around him in the jungle, his twenty comrades. They waited for a signal from Andres, their man on the inside. This operation took months to plan; it began when Raffi revealed the whereabouts of the secret entrance to Manuel Carrel's compound. Northern Brazil Security's most talented recruit, a young man called Andres had gained the trust of Agg Carrel and bluffed his way into becoming one of the drug lord's sentries. Tonight he must wait until the drug lord and his inner circle retired, disable the alarm in the tunnel, and alert Frankie's team. Upon a signal from Frankie's men, Jaco's team would mount a diversionary attack at the front of the compound.

As he waited, Frankie recollected when a young kitchen hand in Rio and her boyfriend fell victim to his savagery. The boyfriend had pissed off the drug lord's son, his punishment was to have all his fingers broken and then witness as Agg and two thugs raped his girlfriend. The sight of that bright, happy girl so wretched and defeated, Frankie had never forgotten. His hoped for vengeance would not restore the girl's happiness but Frankie felt sure, when she heard Agg was dead, some peace would return to her life. Agg was the only person he intended to kill that night.

The green, night-vision image of the guard at the tunnel entrance showed his struggle to stay awake, his head nodded where he sat with his back to the rock wall. He periodically rose and stamped his feet to kick-start his circulation. Frankie wished he could do the same; his legs numbed. The rhythmic chant of crickets would likely lull him asleep too if it weren't for the clashing songs of a myriad of other insects; it seemed every six legged creature for miles around sought to get laid. Faint Mariachi and static issued from the guard's radio and from somewhere above the descending flute notes of a potoo echoed intermittently across the mountainside. Frankie tried to ignore the dampness of his head inside the hazmat communication helmet; the bulletproof vest inside the black combat gear rubbed his hips—he loathed wearing such articles, but in operations like this, they proved indispensable. He preferred his international standard chef's uniform any day.

A sudden yowl fractured the silence of midnight on the mountainside, raising the hackles of the waiting mercenaries. The lamp like eyes of an ocelot gleamed through the vegetation; the cat stared in Frankie's direction for a minute before it melted into the night.

Frankie's heart leapt as the timepiece on his arm vibrated. He winced as he watched the advance party silently approach the dozing sentry; they disarmed, bound and gagged him before the man could raise the alarm.

"Clear."

"One."

The words sounded in Frankie's ear and he got to his feet.

"Two. Three…"

On each count, a man rose and advanced to the tunnel; one by one, they slipped inside.

"Nadie."

"Clear."

The advance moved into the black shaft. They proceeded warily on the rough-hewn stairs of the old silver mine—down and down.

"Hold." The man spoke in a whisper.

Frankie could hear no sound other than the footsteps of his team and the tinkle of water trickling down the rock walls; a faint glow in his night vision goggles heralded another possible sentry post.

"Clear."

An occasional dislodged stone and a snap of rat bones underfoot the only sounds. They proceeded down for fifty-five minutes before the tunnel levelled out.

"Hold."

The advance established the absence of hostile forces ahead. A leapfrogging progression wasn't an option in this narrow tunnel, and unnecessary—they exercised caution but encountered none after the guard at the entrance.

"Nadie."

"Clear."

They followed as the tunnel widened into a cavern the size of an average suburban house, tiny bones crunched under their feet: rodents, bats, and reptile bones—their stench hung stale in the darkness. They stayed close and continued into another opening and fifteen minutes later, the tunnel began to rise. Excitement and tension surged in

Frankie's chest, adrenaline rose with each step—he could feel his erection growing and cursed to himself. Why did an anticipated fight always give him a hard-on? It would soon deflate in the heat of battle. Frankie's heartbeat rose with each step, up and up.

After two hours in the tunnel, they reached the top of the stairs and entered a room with concrete block walls joined to the mountain. A rivulet trickled down the mountain and disappeared into a grate. Carrel had spared no expense when he constructed this compound. A dim crack of light showed around a door. Andres had only been able to give them a partial map of what lay beyond. The timepiece on Frankie's wrist vibrated again—his team's signal to the men out front they had arrived.

"Hold."

The door opened a crack, the leader listened, an alarm sounded and they heard shouts and running feet as Carrel's men responded. Jaco's men had begun their assault at the front.

"Nadie."

"Hold."

They waited as most of the occupants scrambled to defend the compound; Frankie's damp hands tightened their grip on the AAC Honey Badger.

"Go! Go! Go!"

Their guns held ready to fire, the advance made a quick sweep of the room, behind furniture, behind curtains and in cupboards.

"Nadie!"

"Nadie!"

"Clear!"

As Frankie entered the ornate central room he turned left and his division of five men, Silvio, Pio, Val, Jule and a fierce young Tibetan called Tenzin followed. Alfonso's division went to the right and the remaining ten proceeded towards the front of the casa where the clamour of battle echoed. A closed door at the end of the room Frankie knew led to Carrel's bedroom. A sleep-befuddled man blocked their path.

"Lie down!" Frankie spoke in English and Silvio translated. The man hesitated and Frankie poked the Honey Badger at his face, he dropped to the floor, the rear guard quickly bound and gagged him.

Pedro shoved back the door from where their prisoner had emerged and hastened around the room, checking wardrobes and behind curtains.

"Nadie."

As his men moved into the next room, Frankie hurried further along the corridor and opened the door. Manuel Carrel switched on the bed lamp.

"Get your hands up!"

He groped under his pillow and Frankie fired two shots into the drug lord's chest and one shot to the head, blood and brains sprayed across the bed head and up the wall. His bed mate screamed.

"Get out."

A teenage girl scrambled to her feet and covered her nakedness with a bathrobe. Her dark eyes large in her blood splattered face.

"Out!" Frankie motioned with his head towards the door.

"Take her away and cuff her!" he called to Silvio. He leaned over and checked Carrel's neck for a pulse. Dead. Frankie wiped the blood from his fingers on Carrel's sheet and lifted the corner of his pillow, the dead hand loosely held a Glock 19. He froze at a sound behind him and the cool muzzle of a gun pressed against his neck.

"Drop it."

Frankie stuck his left hand in the air and allowed the Honey Badger to spin inverse in his right, as if he might drop it, the muzzle poked against the man and Frankie squeezed the trigger. With only his finger and thumb to check the recoil the volley peppered wildly down his screaming opponent's leg. A single bullet pierced the air as Frankie dived, rolled and regained his grip on the Honey Badger. Prone, he hunted for his assailant. His eyes found Agg Carrel as his leg crumpled under him. The Honey Badger fired again and Agg died before he hit the floor.

"Frankie!" Silvio burst into the room, his gun held ready; his eyes darted from Agg to Manuel then on to Frankie. "Are we taking no prisoners?"

"We are, just nobody told these two."

As Frankie and Silvio emerged from Carrel's bedroom, Val and Tenzin secured the last of the prisoners from that section of the casa.

"All clear! Move out. Pio and Jule remain with the prisoners." Frankie's part in this fight ended with the death of Agg Carrel but he'd never desert his comrades.

It took thirty minutes to secure Carrel's compound. The flutter of Chinooks sounded in the distance; Northern Brazil Security's clean-up team approached to remove the prisoners.

Andres had identified the man before Frankie as one of Carrel's inner circle. He nudged his head with the muzzle of the Honey Badger.

"Where is Santiago Mazo?" He waited for Silvio to translate.

"He says he's not here."

"I know he's not here, where the fuck is he?"

"He's away."

"Where?" Frankie fired a round into the ground beside the man.

"El jefe lo envió a Australia!"

"Say what?"

"He said the boss sent him to Australia."

"When?"

"Cuando?"

"Ayer."

"He said yesterday."

"Cheers mate." Frankie ruffled the man's hair.

<h1 style="text-align:center">41</h1>

Dylan hoped Kate would never discover he'd visited Heather. Ollie's beautiful wife was four years older than Dylan. This wouldn't be the first time Dylan had come calling when Ollie was abroad. He overheard Shirley bragging to one of her high society friends that Oliver was in China on a trade mission for four days; he would return Sunday.

"Dylan!" Heather's pretty, botox frozen face turned pink and Dylan watched her nipples hardened behind the fine jersey fabric or her top. "You were a naughty boy on Wednesday, disrupting Ollie's speech like that."

Dylan stepped through the door and closed it behind him. "I had a dash of hay fever, I couldn't help it." The back of his fingers skimmed her nipple.

She jerked in a gasp of air. "So why are you here?"

"Do you even have to ask?" He pulled her against him and took a bite of her collagen-filled lips then forced them apart with his tongue. Her arms slipped around his neck, her leg wound about his. Silicone-filled breasts gouged his chest. "Crack open a Moet—it's been too long."

"You're the expert barman, you do it while I slip into something more comfortable."

She took him through to Ollie's plush party room— carpet thick enough to muffle screams—walls painted in shades of stone, duck egg, and fuck you.

Opulent wankery.

Dylan went behind the bar, selected the most expensive bottle of champagne and found two long stem glasses. He took the small pack of powder from his pocket and tipped it into one of the glasses. In his brother's bedroom, he poured champagne over the powder and held the fizzing drink to Heather's lips. He watched her take a long swig, she had always been one for quaffing alcohol like there was no tomorrow. She dressed in a transparent, lacy negligee and French knickers, a remarkable sight.

That's my girl, the porn star.

Heather Jackson, the daughter of a wealthy property developer, educated at an exclusive girl's school and then sent to a Swedish finishing school to ready her for high society; only Dylan knew her wild side. He'd had an on and off affair with his sister-in-law since she began dating Ollie at university. On her wedding night, Dylan had proposed a toast to the bride and groom. Later, he lifted the white silk and lace of her bridal gown and screwed her against the wall in a dark alleyway.

Come—drink up, Cherie. I don't have all day.

The last pale golden drop disappeared between her juicy lips as she drained the glass and held it out for a refill, her eyes never leaving his. He poured her another and she guzzled half. Dylan moved closer pulling her against him, this was an exercise in deception but his cock knew no better. She knelt before him, freed it from his jeans and licked it like a Chocolate Billabong. He took two handfuls of her platinum blond hair and forced himself into her throat. She moaned and sucked. Dylan pulled her to her feet, stripped off her flimsy garments and pushed her back onto the bed; she opened her legs. He tipped the fizzing drink into her and licked it out; she giggled and sighed.

More slopped over her breasts and he licked it off; she whimpered and wailed. He poured the champagne into her mouth, his tongue helped swish it over her tonsils then he leaned back on the bed head—she knew the drill. She climbed onto his lap and impaled herself on him, her erect nipples brushed across his face; he caught one in his mouth and lightly bit then licked.

Ollie, you inadequate little cunt—I could take your wife away in a heartbeat.

His hands almost encircled her waist as he pushed deeper into her, she squealed and moaned with each orgasm—one, then two, then another—Dylan decided three was all he'd give her, he pushed her back on the pillows and straddled her. He grasped her tits, wedged himself between them and with a few thrusts he cum on to her collarbone.

"Why didn't I marry you, Dylan?"

"Because I didn't ask you?"

"No, I married Ollie because my parents said he was going to be the successful one."

"Yes, he's much more successful than the little brother who fucks his wife anytime he wants."

"Dylan, you're such a gorgeous big stud. You know you could make a fortune as a gigolo." She giggled and kissed his chest.

"Most of the women I fuck couldn't afford to pay me."

"I know of at least five women who have plenty of money, they all want you to fuck them."

"I only fuck the pretty ones."

Dylan knew which women she spoke of, they often came to Raffi's with their dumb-fuck husbands. While their husbands swigged their boutique beer, slapped each other's prosperous backs and paid tribute to one another's business prowess, their wives licked their expensive lips and made eyes at Dylan. Dylan Delaney, the alcoholic younger brother of Oliver Jackson MP. Dylan Delaney, tall and sexy—the handsomest man in Sydney society—and a failure. Loser—or so they all thought.

And they're probably right but still, I could be fucking their wives six ways to Sunday.

The crushed Valium had taken effect. Heather slept, sprawled out naked, his semen shining on her smooth skin and champagne stains soaked the expensive cotton sheets.

Dylan got to his feet and dressed. He grabbed the half-empty champagne bottle by the neck and began searching his brother's house. Two hours later, he admitted defeat. He progressed to his mother's house and began searching again. She wasn't home, he knew where she went this afternoon—to Newcastle to open a library in the absence of her son, Oliver. Dylan smiled.

Newcastle—if only its people remembered Shirley from her younger days.

The library didn't exist, nor did the address on the invitation but by the time Shirley Jackson woke to the fact she'd been pranked, Dylan would have finished riffling through all the cupboards and hidey-holes in her house. In a plastic container of photos and documents, he found something he wasn't looking for; a sealed stationary box, with his mother's handwriting; *'Diaries 1994-5 and 6 and those videos. (My insurance).'*

He tucked it under his arm and continued his search; he found what he searched for in the last place he looked—the manhole. As soon as he poked his head into the ceiling, he saw it; a dusty shoebox with a perished rubber band stretched around it. He used a pen to break the rubber band and lift the lid.

So, this is what you did with it, you slimy fucking snake.

He pulled a Gladbag from his pocket, slipped it over the box, closed the manhole, and climbed down.

****

Sitting in the back of a Silver Top, flicking through Shirley's diaries, Dylan had his eyes opened wide. He arrived at Raffi's House of Blues and found Raffi cleaning the glass-fridge doors behind the bar, the purr of the glass washer came to a dripping halt as Dylan pulled up a barstool.

"Rum?" said Raffi.

"Yep, I'm giving it up tomorrow."

"For real?"

"For real."

"What brought that on?"

"I'm about to grass up my mother and brother; I'm going to need my wits about me."

"What's that?" Raffi pointed to the gladbag Dylan had set on the bar top.

"Some long lost deadly secrets, I searched Shirley's and Ollie's house and found them."

"How did you get to search Ollie's house?"

Questions like this reminded Dylan that Raffi was only twenty-four years old—still wet behind the ears. He grinned, "I have ways."

"Yeah," Raffi shook his head, "I don't want to know. So what is it in there?"

"The first thing Ollie will go looking for if he thinks I'm talking to the police."

"So when are you going to the police?"

"Solicitor—first thing Monday, little Bro. Lloyd is taking me to a friend of his who is a good criminal lawyer. Then the shit will really hit the fan."

"Why the delay?"

"Ollie is out of the country, we want him here in Australia when the police go to arrest him. Have you got that sleek new car of yours here?"

"Parked out the back."

"Give me a ride over to Elizabeth Street."

"Say please?"

"I say give me a ride and next week, I'll become your bar manager. That's if they don't throw me in the clink."

Pain flashed across Raffi's handsome face; Dylan thought his mention of prison might have brought back a painful memory.

"What does Lloyd say? Does he think you'll be sent down?"

"He's optimistic—but I'm not. Raffi, has Mia mentioned me?"

Raffi bit his lip and shook his head.

"She hasn't said much about it, I think she's still trying to come to terms with finding out who her father is."

"I want to take back what I did to her mother but at the same time, I'm proud to be her father even if I can never claim the honour." Dylan's throat hurt with the tears he had yet to shed. "A beautiful girl like her deserves a father she could love and be proud of, but instead, she got me."

"You're doing the right thing, Dylan. You're taking steps to make it right."

"They're steps I would have taken years ago if I'd only known she existed."

42

Scott Matthews set his computer on to record.

"Okay, tell me, Dylan. Take it from the beginning—are you sure you don't want to talk to a counsellor first?"

Scott sat down opposite the handsome younger brother of Oliver Jackson. He bored no resemblance to his more famous brother and his reputation for drinking and carousing legendary. The shadows under his eyes gave him a tired appearance. When Scott's friend and colleague, Lloyd Beaufort called him and told him Dylan Delaney needed a lawyer, that he wanted to spill the beans on his politician brother, Matthew had laughed, but when Lloyd gave him a hint of what it entailed, Scott grew excited.

"Yeah, I'm sure." Dylan sighed and slumped back in his chair. "From the beginning?"

"It's a good place to start."

Dylan chewed his lip a moment and inhaled.

"Okay. The first time I thought there was something amiss with my brother was when he tortured the neighbour's cat."

Scott frowned. "Go on."

"Kitten actually. It used to come over into our yard—I would have been about seven or eight, Ollie was about twelve maybe thirteen. On this morning, I dragged a piece of rope around on the grass and the kitten chased it. I loved cats and my mother hated them, she wouldn't let me have one. Anyway, Ollie came out and saw me. He came over and picked up the kitten."

****

"He's a cute little fella isn't he, Dylan?"

"Yeah, he's funny."

"You like playing with him, don't you?"

"Yeah."

"Only poofters like cats. You're a fag, Dylan."

"I'm not!" Dylan's stomach churned—sometimes his brother was nice, other times, scary.

"I'll show you how boys play with cats."

Ollie stepped over to the Hill's Hoist and grabbed a handful of pegs from Shirley's laundry trolley. Dylan watched in horror as Ollie pegged the kitten by the skin of his back to the clothesline. Five pegs held the screaming kitten to the line, Ollie pegged its tail to the line as well.

"Stop it!" Dylan ran to help the kitten and Ollie punched him in the solar plexus. He fell to the ground gasping in pain.

"Yeah go on, cry you little poofter! Faggot! Nobody's going to hear you."

The one thing at which Ollie excelled was pitching. He could throw with deadly accuracy and with the power of a baseball pitcher. As Dylan sobbed, Ollie began pelting marbles at the kitten, when he ran out of those he threw rocks from a nearby garden at it until the struggling kitten popped the last of the pegs off and it fled under the fence, its tail bent at an odd angle.

****

"I never saw that kitten again." Dylan rubbed his hand over his face and sat up straight. "Then there was the time we visited our paternal grandmother. She had a budgerigar in a cage on the back veranda. I was about eight or nine and I guess Ollie was about thirteen."

Dylan's eyes found Scott's.

"I loved watching the little budgie, he would come to the bars and chatter to me and nibble my fingers."

****

"What, playing with the cute little birdie, Dylan?" Ollie mocked his younger brother. "Getting your faggot on?"

"Go away!"

Ollie kicked Dylan's legs from under him; he fell hard.

"Don't tell me to go away you little queer. You like the little tweety bird, do you?" Ollie hit the cage; the tiny bird screeched and ruffled his feathers.

"Leave him alone!"

"Birds have lice, did you know that, Faggot?"

"He hasn't got lice; Grandma takes good care of him."

"This is how you treat lice, Dylan." Ollie grabbed a can of Baygon off the windowsill and poked the spray straw through the bars and squirted the insecticide into the budgie's face. The little bird fell to the floor of the cage, its pitiful squeaks faded, its fluttering wings slowed to twitches. Ollie laughed as the bird went still.

"I'm Louie the Fly, I'm Louie the Fly…" he sang and chased Dylan with the spray can, squirting it at him. Dylan ran to his grandmother.

****

"Would you like to stop for a while, Dylan?"

"No, I have to get this over with."

"Would you like a drink?"

"Mate, I love a drink, but I'm trying hard to give it up. I don't want some smartarse defence barrister accusing me of being an alcoholic."

"Okay then, we'll continue with the next horror story. Christ, Dylan, I've heard stories that Oliver Jackson is an arsehole but I bet no one knows the full extent of it."

"I do. So does my mother, Shirley. I'll get to her next." Dylan ran his fingers through his hair and squinted at the ceiling.

"One day, I followed him when we were at the beach—I used to follow him everywhere—I was about ten. I saw him ahead of me, he ran out of the sand dunes and down to the beach. I had to run to catch up to him and I ran past a girl lying in the sand—about fifty metres from me, half-naked and crying. Hysterical and bleeding. I never heard if a rape was reported—I was just a little kid—but I'm sure that's what he did. It had to be him—there was no one else around. I would be willing to bet that was the first girl he raped."

Dylan shifted in his seat, his hand shook as he raised his glass of water to his mouth. He held it in front of him and continued.

"Then a few years later, he beat the crap out of me, I was about twelve I think. He would have been sixteen or seventeen and he came in one night, Mum was at work or out on the town, I don't know—I was home alone—yeah I know; she often used to leave me by myself. It must have been close to midnight and Ollie came in the back door. I woke up and went to see who it was. He was sweaty and winded as if he had ran a long way. He had a scratch on his face and blood all down the leg of his jeans; I asked him what happened. He got angry and told me to mind my own fucking business. I asked him if he been hurting more animals and he punched me in the guts. I curled up in a ball on the floor and he kicked me a half a dozen times." He exhaled and set the glass back on the desk.

"He put his jeans in the wash along with his joggers and shirt—he must have set it on a long cycle because I went back to bed and woke hours later and it was still washing.

"The next day, it was all over the news that a girl named Tahnee had been raped and murdered down at Cronulla. When he saw me watching it he got me by the throat and told me he would kill me if I said anything to anyone about the bloody jeans. He smacked me around, gave me a black eye and did his usual abuse—you know— called me a faggot. Fucking Shirley staggered through to the kitchen and told Ollie not to hit me too hard. Fucking old moll—"

Dylan sniffed and Scott was unsurprised to see tears on his cheeks. "You're doing well, Dylan. Just take all the time you need."

"There was a spate of them about a year later, three girls in a row—raped and murdered in the same way. When they found the second one, the police were saying they searched for one man, a serial killer—the papers began calling him 'The Sand Dune Killer' because two of the girls they found in the sand dunes. He must have gotten better at it because I never saw any more blood on his clothes."

Dylan fell silent, deep in thought; Scott waited. The undulant traffic hum continued on Elizabeth Street far below.

"I hero-worshipped my big brother, even with all the abuse I took from him. Some perverse part of my brain thought it was my fault when he abused me, when he beat me up. I was even convinced I must have been gay, although I liked girls, I could never have imagined getting it on with a boy."

Dylan sighed and squeezed his eyes shut.

"We can take a break if you want—"

He shook his head as if to shake off a persistent fly.

"Then Mum, me, and Ollie went to Bundeena for a week's holiday."

It occurred to Scott that Dylan might have forgotten he was there.

"It was May or June in ninety-four. Mum rented a unit down there. About four days after we got there, Ollie and me took a walk to the beach. It was fairly late in the afternoon and we went through what I later found out was a national park."

****

"Hey, Dylan. Take a look at this little sweetie."

Dylan could see a girl of a similar age to himself approaching along the narrow path through the scrub.

"You want to fuck her don't you?" Ollie gave Dylan a shove.

"No."

"No? Faggot—go on, prove you're not a poofter."

"I don't even know her. I can't—"

"I will, look and learn." Ollie breathed hard and squeezed his crotch; Dylan could see he had an erection. "I'm not a poof; I'm going to fuck her."

"No don't!"

The girl surveyed the path behind her and didn't see the man approach. Ollie clamped his hand over her mouth and dragged her into a thick patch of scrub.

"Come on; prove you're not a poofter."

"No! Ollie don't!" Dylan pushed through the undergrowth, hoping Ollie would let the girl go, hoping Ollie was joking. His heart thudded as Ollie tackled the girl to the ground and ripped off her bikini top.

"No!" the girl wailed, "Please, let me go!"

"Nice tits!"

The girl screamed and Ollie punched her senseless. He pulled off her sarong and bikini bottom and Dylan got his first live view of a naked girl. Ollie opened his fly and lowered himself over her.

"Aw Jesus—she's a virgin." He muttered and clamped his hand over her mouth as he penetrated her. She made muffled, high-pitched noises as Ollie forced himself into her and began thrusting hard and fast. Dylan's whole *body grew hot as blood pulsed a fusion of fear and lust through his veins. Dizzy—in a dream sequence, he opened his jeans and freed his throbbing erection. Ollie growled and bit the girl's shoulder; he panted, slamming his hips against the girl's groin—once—twice—and—*

"Ah fuck!"

Dylan didn't know an erection could hurt and his throbbed painfully. Ollie pushed him on top of the dazed girl.

"Go on! Prove you're not a poof."

On his knees between the girl's legs, Dylan shivered; Ollie shoved his shoulder again. "Go on, faggot! Stick your cock into her." He smacked the back of Dylan's head.

Dylan penetrated the girl, he couldn't stop, he thrust into her. It felt good—and bad—Dylan felt sick. Over in less than a minute, he stumbled to his feet and reality returned. He was now a rapist, like his brother. Tears fell down his face as he vomited into the grass.

The sobbing girl fought to regain her feet and Ollie lifted the rock over his head; the word tore from Dylan's throat.

****

The big man sobbed like a child; mucus and tears poured from his face. Scott found himself weeping with him. He moved around the desk to sit beside him, his arm across Dylan's heaving shoulders; how could he comfort such distress.

"That rock was bigger than a fucking football! Before I could do anything, Ollie threw it at her head. You should have—ah Christ—you—it left a dent in the back of her head! A dent an inch deep—" Dylan's voice faded to a hoarse whisper.

"It's okay, Dylan—you don't have to go on. We have enough to put that bastard away for life." Scott dragged a handful of tissues from the box on his desk and handed them to Dylan, then grabbed a few for himself.

"I don't remember walking back to the unit. I know I vomited everywhere. Ollie punched me in the guts like he always did. Have you ever been hit in the guts when you're not expecting it? It knocks the life out of you. It fucking hurts! You can't breathe—you feel sick."

"Dylan, we can take a break—"

"We got back to the unit and I got in the shower and stayed there for an hour. When I came out, it was all over the TV. They had found the girl, barely alive—raped and left for dead. Ollie was pleased—can you believe that? He laughed—said the police were dickheads. That arsehole was proud of himself! I was terrified—the girl's little sister had seen us. She told the police about the stupid tattoo Ollie had on his hand. I went to bed that night thinking I was going to jail. When I got up in the morning Ollie was gone. I didn't know how at the time, I found out a week later that Shirley got him out of there. She had one of her dodgy friends that owned a boat, nip down from Sydney and pick him up in the middle of the night. She got some creepy bikie friend of hers to come around and removed the tattoo on Ollie's hand. My mother covered up what we did.

"Somehow she scared Ollie into changing his ways—not long after that he went to university and he never raped any more girls that I know of. He began to call himself Oliver Jackson—he hated it when anyone called him Ollie—it seemed to make him nervous. He dropped the surname, Delaney."

"Can you remember who removed the tattoo?"

Dylan shook his head and ran a shaking hand over his face.

"No."

"It's okay—the police may be able to track the guy down."

"That girl—Rosie Colter—she became pregnant. She was brain damaged and blind from the blow to her head, but she conceived a child; she gave birth to my daughter and then they turned off the life support, Rosie died shortly after. My daughter's name is Mia. She's beautiful. I wish I was good enough to call myself her father." Dylan sniffed and wept into a soggy tissue.

"Lloyd told me about how she worked out who you were."

Dylan laughed through his tears. "She's a clever girl, she figured it out. I'm glad she did. Even if I go to jail, I'm glad she figured it out."

"Well, you've done the right thing, Dylan—"

"What a pity I didn't tell the police of my suspicions that night he came home with blood on his pants. I might have saved the rest of those girls—"

"You were a child, Dylan. You can't blame yourself for what happened."

"But I do. I shouldn't have let him rape Rosie Colter."

"You were a fourteen-year-old kid. He was eighteen—a grown man. How could you have stopped him?"

"I should have tried—I should have run away—I thought if I stayed he wouldn't hurt her. No, I could not—even—he was always so aggressive! I was a weak little bastard. Even now, I hate fighting—Pat—my stepfather taught me to defend myself. Pat made me strong but the older I get the less I can carry it off.

"Ollie has a certain kind of charm. I don't know—I can charm my way into the pants of almost any woman I look at, that's something Ollie can't do. But other men like him, the voters like him—they think he's a good bloke. When a disaster strikes Oliver Jackson is always there with his sleeves rolled up, shovel in hand. Cunt. His favourite trick is to breast the bar with the blokes and show them what a man he is—skol a beer—tell a dirty joke. Cunt. He's a lowlife cunt!"

Scott watch Dylan, slumped in his chair, hands covering his face he took a shuddering breath.

"I might be inclined to forgive him if I thought he'd really changed, but he hasn't. You should hear him and Mum having a good old laugh at Ollie's parliamentary colleagues or just the average voter. He likes to sit back and heap shit on the people on welfare, he puts in a lot of time lecturing us all on how we should take care of the less fortunate. Trust me; he only says that shit to get votes. He doesn't give a flying fuck about those poor buggers in public housing. Shirley—only last Christmas, full of booze and bad manners, said Ollie should organise a cull of Western Sydney. They had a good old laugh. Ollie said it was a good idea, I seriously think he wasn't joking—if he could get away with it, he would."

43

Lloyd collected a couple of files from his assistant's desk and headed for his office. The door pushed open and Scott Matthews entered.

"Lloyd, I need a drink, something of very high octane."

"Sure, come in."

Red eyed and pale, Scott slumped into the chair beside Lloyd's desk and rubbed his face with both hands.

"What was the name of that detective, the one who led the investigation into the Sand Dune Killer?"

"Will Fishman." Lloyd poured Cognac into two glasses of ice. "He's over at the police headquarters these days. He's a Superintendent or—something like that. Stephanie is his assistant."

"Have I got some good news for him? Oliver Jackson is going to be toast."

"Dylan told all?"

Scott nodded. "Poor bastard. How unlucky to be born with a mother and brother like that pair."

Lloyd sat the glass of Cognac in front of Scott and moved around the desk to his chair.

"You recorded it?"

"Yeah, he was okay with me recording it. I think he hopes it will save him from having to tell the story a second time." Scott took a mouthful of Cognac and swallowed. He coughed and croaked, "I wish I could tell him he won't have to, but I think he's got a lot of telling to do yet."

"I wish I could listen to it but given my relationship to Mia, it's best if I stay right out of it. So when are you going to see Fishman?"

"As soon as I can make an appointment."

Lloyd picked up his phone. "Anne, can you see if you can get Superintendent Fishman's assistant on the line for me? Yeah. Thanks."

Lloyd lounged back and took a sip of his drink; Scott drank his in gulps and coughed with each swallow. Presently the phone trilled and Lloyd snatched it up.

"What's this about, Lloyd? Superintendent Fishman is a busy man."

"He's not too busy for this, Stephanie. Can I speak to him?"

"Tell me what it's about and I'll see if he can spare you a minute."

"It's about Rosie Colter."

Lloyd heard a scuffle on the other end and a squeak of alarm from Stephanie.

"You better not be shitting me, Beaufort." Will Fishman's voice had a sandpapered edge.

"I have a colleague here who has just heard a confession from the Sand Dune Killer's accomplice. He has enough information for you to hang the guy."

"If only we did still hang them, Beaufort. Where will I find this colleague of yours?"

"On the tenth floor of my building in Elizabeth Street. Scott Matthews, Solicitors."

"I'll be there as soon as possible; hopefully the traffic is not too heavy. Is this accomplice still there?"

Lloyd's head swivelled to Scott who shook his head. "No, I think he went home."

"What? He should be in custody!"

"He came forward of his own volition, Superintendent, he's not going to suddenly leave town."

"Right! I'll be right over."

"Superintendent, before you go. Not a word to anyone, okay. The Sand Dune Killer is a VIP in this State. Tell Stephanie to keep quiet, I'm serious."

"I'll be over shortly."

****

"Jesus, Steff! Why do you wear those bloody high heels?" Will Fishman growled impatiently at his assistant as she teetered behind him, wearing five-inch heels. "Just as well we're not chasing down a crook!"

"Sorry, Will, but you are walking awfully fast."

"Girl," he muttered, "I spent the last twenty odd years grinding my teeth to stubs over this case. I hope this pair of pansy lawyers know what they're doing."

Fishman stamped into the lift and held the doors open for his assistant then poked the tenth floor button using the philosophy the harder you press the faster they will respond. As the doors inched closed, Will took several deep, calming breaths. He centred his nose where the doors met, ready to launch himself through when they opened.

****

Scott waited by his receptionist's desk until Fishman arrived.

"Superintendent Fishman, please come in. Hello Stephanie, how is life in the police service?"

"Hi, Scott, it's—"

"What have you got for me, Matthews?"

Scott smiled at Stephanie and closed the door. Stephanie had worked upstairs for Beaufort, Jones, and Associates for several years before she landed her dream job in the police department.

"Take a seat, Superintendent." He pulled out at chair for Stephanie and moved around to sit behind his desk. "I heard a confession today, from Dylan Delaney."

"Dylan Delaney? I've heard that name. What—keep going."

"You know Oliver Jackson? Dylan's his brother."

"Oliver Jackson!" Fishman's eyebrows shot up into his hairline.

"He's your man."

"Okay, we do need to tread wary, he's a personal friend of the commissioner. Let me see what you've got."

Scott opened his laptop, tapped the keyboard and rolled the video. He turned the computer around for Fishman and Stephanie to watch.

Fifty minutes later, both Fishman and his assistant wiped tears from their eyes.

"Can I get a copy of this, Scott?" Fishman wiped a shaking hand over his face.

Scott opened his desk drawer, took out a flash-drive and handed it across.

"Jackson is a flight risk, Superintendent. Dylan is worried as soon as he finds out he's going to be arrested he's likely to leave the country. The sooner you can arrest him the better."

"Stephanie, contact the boys in blue and tell them to bring him in. Tell them to send the higher ranks, and tell them if he's in the parliamentary precinct they'll need to notify the presiding officer or the speaker—they should know that anyway. And tell them, no chatter! This needs to be kept quiet until he's in custody!" Fishman got to his feet. "I better call the assist-commish. This is going to ruffle some very important feathers."

"I'll bring Dylan to the headquarters tomorrow morning. Don't worry, he's not going to take off anywhere. He wants to see his brother behind bars."

"What a shame he didn't think that way twenty years ago."

"Well, he was a kid and you heard—"

"Yeah."

44

Oliver Jackson stared, transfixed by the video footage from the camera he'd installed in his bedroom. Anger burned his guts as he watched his petite wife climb onto his brother's cock.

This has been going on for years, hasn't it?

He remembered on his wedding night as he went down on her, he thought he tasted another man's semen. Had Dylan fucked her on their wedding night?

And what about that night when in the throes of an orgasm, she called his name?

At the time Ollie told himself he only imagined hearing her cry, "Dylan!"

Several times in the past, Ollie had found it amusing his little brother had screwed several of his political party member's wives, now he knew—while he laughed at them,

Dylan cuckolded him as well. Dylan Delaney—widely regarded as The Stud of Surry Hills. The Rooster of Rushcutters Bay. The Cock of King's Cross. His little brother had earned legendary status and numerous monikers. Men secretly wished they could be him, he could charm his way into the bed of any woman he wanted. Big—and watching this video he could see just how big—and impossibly handsome. Ollie knew Dylan wasn't wealthy, he didn't seem to care about money—women didn't care either. They simply wanted his undivided attention and a chance to share his bed.

"I should have knocked you on the head with a rock when you were a skinny kid, you cheating fucking bastard."

The notion of knocking someone on the head with a rock made Ollie's penis stand like a flagpole. He switched off the video as he heard Heather's car in the garage. He met her as she came through the door and slapped her hard up the side of the head.

"You fucking bitch!"

She screamed as she hit the floor. Ollie grabbed a fistful of her hair and dragged her to the bedroom.

"You let my brother into our bed! You two-timing whore!"

"Ollie, stop!"

He ripped her dress from her shoulders and tore her bra away. Heather tried to escape as he swung again, his fist caught her under the jaw, he thought he heard a bone crack. He fell on top of her, his forearm across her throat. His breathing ragged as he hooked his arm behind her knee, forced it up to her shoulder and held it under the weight of his body.

"You fucked my brother!" The flimsy knickers tore easily and he guided himself into her and began thrusting hard, he pinched her to make her cry out. Her cries made him rock-hard. "That's right, scream! It's how you like it, isn't it?"

"No!"

"You like my brother's cock?"

"Don't! You're hurting!"

Ollie's teeth sank into the shoulder of his sobbing wife. "I like hurting women, didn't know that did you?" He bit her breast and tasted blood, "Like that? Admit it, you like it!"

"No—stop!"

"All these years I've been treating you gently, like a romantic schoolboy and all you wanted was my brother's cock! Well take some of mine! Take it hard!"

She pushed him off and rolled away, Ollie grabbed a handful of hair and yanked her head back; he enjoyed the sensation of her soft skin yielding to his pounding fists. His knee forced her legs apart, he entered her anally, thrusting hard and fast; He growled and bit her shoulder as the orgasm shook his body.

He left her sobbing and bleeding on the floor and went back to his den. He checked the other security camera footage—Dylan had searched his house.

"You bastard," he whispered. He knew what he sought. Ollie smiled his secret smile, his brother could search for a year and he wouldn't find his trophies. Shirley had told Ollie to destroy his trophy box but he hadn't. He stored it in Shirley's ceiling. Even if anyone found it, they wouldn't know its significance.

The sudden trill of the phone startled him out of his reverie.

"Dylan is going to the cops."

Bile rose in Ollie's throat, he swallowed hard and couldn't speak, Shirley sounded so sure.

"Ollie?"

"Bullshit, Mum, he'd have to turn himself in to do that."

"He's speaking to a lawyer."

"How do you know?"

"I've had Grennie follow him. He searched my house, he's looking for that box of yours, I'm sure he is. I hope you destroyed it like I told you to."

"Sure, Mum—of course I did." Ollie's shaking hand jiggled the receiver against his ear; his skin prickled and crawled.

"I'm putting Grennie and his men onto it."

"Dylan won't go to the cops."

Ollie wished he could be as sure as he knew he sounded. Oliver Jackson was a career politician; he excelled at sounding utterly certain when his heart held nothing but doubts. He turned back to the video and watched Dylan swigging from a Champagne bottle as he riffled through the drawers in this office.

"You know what they say about denial, Ollie…" His mother hung up.

Oliver Jackson swore, had Dylan finally plucked up the courage to defy him? Oliver Jackson?

Galvanised to action, Oliver booted his computer and logged onto Flight Centre dot com. Let Shirley take care of his little brother. He dashed off to his room and packed a suitcase. Where had Heather disappeared? He busied himself gathering what he would need for a long stay in Europe. He would send for Heather to join him when he got there, he didn't have time to wait for her to ready herself.

He swore again, louder this time, as he heard his wife's car start and reverse from the garage. He ran to stop her.

"Heather! Get back here! Now!"

She reversed at speed and bumped over the gutter as she swung out onto the street. Ollie had to jump aside as she accelerated away. He hurried back into the house to grab his suitcase, gather his personal papers and call a cab.

"Eastern Europe, here I come."

45

Mia closed her front door, slipped her keys into her bag and slung the strap across her shoulder. As she set off along the lane into the cold, cloudy afternoon her mind wandered, settled on Raffi, and the attendant guilt bubbled up. She still harboured an ocean of remorse for hurting Christopher. Annoyance twinged her gut—she had never told Christopher she loved him, she never lied to him. Every second she spent fretting over it wasted her precious energy. She turned her thoughts back to Raffi and smiled. He'd come to be her anchor, her stability in a chaotic world. Mia's first love swept her away in a river of joy— body, heart, and spirit. She altered her course to squeeze between the wall and a van parked in her path. Strong arms grabbed her from behind and a sweaty hand clamped over her mouth—her feet dragged across the concrete path as her captor hauled her into the back of a van and the door slammed. A searing flood of adrenaline set her trembling and acid stung her throat. Her body pulsed with terror. Thin cable ties fixed her hands behind her, more secured her ankles; her captor forced her to lie face down on the hard floor.

"Scream and I'll beat the shit out of you." The man sounded familiar.

"What do you want with me? Please, let me go."

"Just stay calm and you'll be okay." He gagged and blindfolded her. "This is what happens when you get mixed up with the Rooneys."

****

Dylan listened to the man's words and froze; he gripped the phone harder.

"We have your wife. You can have her back when you hand over what doesn't belong to you. Bring it tonight to the back dock of Raffi's at nine. If you don't we'll kill her. Don't call the cops or we'll kill her anyway." The three beep hang-up tone sounded in his ear.

****

Raffi wondered why Kate hadn't returned. She went to do the banking at three and hadn't come back. He guessed she had gone home early. He waited for Mia, they had a movie date. The front door buzzer sounded and he went to see who it was.

Nobody was there, but a parcel lay on the step. Raffi picked it up and closed the door. Back at his desk, he tore the package open.

"What the fuck?" A gun. He pulled out the magazine; it had two bullets in it. He sat dead still his heartbeat quickened. Why would someone send him a loaded gun? He picked up the parcel post box and noticed it hadn't gone through the Post Office; it bore no stamp or address. The only writing scrawled *'Raf Cheney.'* A folded note lay among the bubble wrap.

'You will kill Dylan Delaney tonight or we'll kill your Mia. Don't call the cops or she'll die anyway. Further instructions to come.'

Raffi's insides iced.

"Mia!" he grabbed his phone and tapped her number.

An automated female voice. "The person you have called has their mobile switched off."

Raffi's hands shook as he called Luke, Mia's lead guitarist.

"G'day Raffi, what are you up to?"

"I'm looking for Mia—urgently."

"She went out hours ago; I assumed she was going to see you."

"If you see her, tell her to stay home and don't let anyone in the door."

He hung up and contemplated his next move, his heart crashed against his ribs.

Please not Mia.

Raffi jumped to his feet and opened the cupboard with the security system inside. He flicked through the stored imagery and found the footage from the camera at the front of the building. A jerky image of a man, his face obscured by a baseball cap hurried up the stairs and placed a parcel at the door, rang the bell and ran away.

"Fuck!" Raffi slammed the cupboard; the footage offered no clues.

He cast his mind about for a culprit and settled on Shirley and Ollie, this had their prints all over it; they must have received word of Dylan talking to the police. They wouldn't know the truth about Mia's relationship to Dylan. He hoped they wouldn't find out, if they did, Mia wouldn't stand a chance. Raffi picked up his phone and called his father.

46

Pat Rooney answered a knock on his door, for a moment he didn't recognise the man standing there, wringing his hands.

"Hello Pat, long time—no see."

"Dave Aspinall! Come in, Dave."

"No Pat, can we talk?" he hurried down the steps and away, he hid from view between a thick Camellia bush and the house, Pat had no option but to follow.

"Pat, your boy is in grave danger."

"Which one?"

"I heard along the grapevine—there's some bloke from South America here and he's under orders to kill your boy, they're talking about tonight. The boy who did time over there."

"Raffi!"

"That's him. I thought I should tell you, Pat. I owe you a favour from way back. You have to hide the boy or they'll kill him—they'll kill me too for telling you—if they find me."

"Okay, thanks, Dave. I owe you one—have you got somewhere to hide?"

"Yeah mate. I'm fuckin' off up north for a few weeks."

"Good. Here…" Pat pulled out his wallet and removed a wad of fifties. "Pay for your trip."

"Jeez, thanks, Pat. You're a good mate."

"You too, Dave. Take care now."

Pat dashed back into the house, "Antoinette, Honey—get Nic and Patrick, quickly!"

"Why? What's the big hurry?"

"Don't ask, just hurry up."

He rushed them to the car. "Sit in the back." Pat knew one day the privacy screens in the back of his Beemer would come in handy. As he backed out of the driveway, he voice dialled Raffi.

"Dad? I was about to call you—"

"Raffi, where are you?"

"I'm at the club, Dad—"

"Stay there! Don't open the door to anyone, okay?"

"Dad, there's some bad shit happening—"

"Stay put, don't go anywhere!"

"But I have to—"

"Just stay where you are!" he roared at the steering wheel. He hung up and cursed the Monday afternoon traffic.

He voice dialled Frankie, the call tone sounded softly in the BMW's speakers as Pat slowed and stopped for a red light. The call went to Frankie's voice mail and Pat jabbed the phone button on the steering wheel.

****

Raffi listened to the hang-up beeps, wondering what his father knew. Pat rarely shouted at anyone.

Does he know what Shirley and Ollie are doing?

He tried to call Mia again and got the same Telstra message. On the off chance she may have gone to his place, he called his home number and listened to himself on the answering machine. He called Lloyd.

"Raffi, how's things?"

"Lloyd, have you seen Mia?"

"Not since Friday, no."

"Shit!"

"Raffi? What's going on?"

Raffi told Lloyd of the delivery and the instruction to kill Dylan.

"Old Shirley is dangerous, so is Ollie. I think they've got her, Lloyd."

"Okay, stay there, I'll be over shortly."

Raffi hung up and stared blankly at his desk. His phone rang and he grabbed it—he didn't recognise the number or the voice on the other end.

"Ten o'clock tonight, have the back dock open. No cops. Don't forget, Mia's life depends on your cooperation." The hang up beeps made his skin crawl. The door opened and Dylan stepped into the room. His face ashen and anxious.

"Raffi—"

Raffi picked up the gun. "I have instructions to kill you, big brother."

Dylan appeared not to have heard him. Raffi laid the gun back on the desk.

"The shit's hit the fan early, Raffi."

"Yes, I know. They've got Mia."

"They have? Fuck it! They've got Kate too!"

"Shit—this will be your mother's work no doubt."

"Her and Ollie, both I'd say. They want me to give back what I took. They must have worked out that I searched their houses. Too bad, Scott Matthews already has Ollie's box of trinkets."

Raffi jumped to his feet as a person appeared in the door behind Dylan. The blonde's familiar face bore cuts and bruises. Dylan spun around.

"Heather! What happened?"

"Ollie—"

"What did he do?"

"He somehow found out about us and he attacked me, I always knew he was hiding his true nature."

"I'll get that bastard…"

"What do you have on Ollie? I heard him talking to Shirley, they're up to something."

"He'd going down, Heather. Don't go home; is there somewhere else you can go?"

"Yes there is. I just came to warn you, Dylan, they're planning something and Ollie is going to leave the country, I'm sure of it. I checked his browser history and he paid for a one-way ticket to Moscow."

"Gutless arsehole!"

Heather held up her hands as Dylan moved towards her.

"Don't!" She shook her head. "I just came to warn you, they're evil, but I guess you know that. Now I'm going to the police. Goodbye, Dylan—take care."

Dylan didn't speak as he watched her leave.

"Did you lock the back door?" Raffi asked.

"Yeah, but I think Ollie has keys to this place—I guess that's how Heather—"

"Shit! Why didn't you fucking tell me? I would have changed the fucking locks!" Raffi picked up the phone and called Lloyd again.

"I've been too bloody drunk for the last five years to think of anything constructive, let alone remembering who has keys to this place." Dylan rubbed his forehead. "If headaches had a colour, this one would be purple and black."

Raffi listened impatiently to the beeps before Lloyd picked up.

"Lloyd, don't come here. Tell the police to get their arse to the airport, all airports. We've just been told Oliver Jackson has bought a one-way ticket to Moscow."

"Dammit! Thanks Raffi. I'll get right on to it. I know they planned to arrest him this afternoon. Hopefully they've already got him."

"Good luck, Lloyd."

Raffi hung up and rubbed his hands over his face. "I better check that Heather locked that back door properly."

"Where did you get the gun, Raffi?"

"It was delivered to me a half an hour ago with instructions to shoot you."

"Well, you better get on with it."

"Don't be stupid, you know I wouldn't kill you."

"It might be more effective than a Panadol. Man I've got a headache!"

"Well, take a Panadol. I'm not in the business of killing loved ones."

Raffi picked up the gun and took it with him. As he hurried through the main clubroom, he tried to quell the rising panic, terror at what might befall Mia tore at him like a waking nightmare.

47

Pat pulled his car in beside Raffi's into the double garage at the back of Raffi's House of Blues. He rushed Antoinette and the boys up the stairs and into the loading dock. The sight that greeted him both relieved and alarmed him.

"Where did you get that from?" he demanded.

Raffi held a handgun pointed at the ceiling.

"Whoa!" Nic's eyes widened, "where did you get that?"

"Raffi! What…" Antoinette began to berate her son but Pat waved at her to be quiet.

"A present from your good wife, Dad."

"It's a long time since I considered her my wife, Raffi." He hugged his son. "Boy, I'm glad to see you."

"Dad—"

"There's some hit man from Colombia here in Sydney, he's come to get you, Raffi." Antoinette gave a cry of alarm, "Shh girl! No one is going to hurt our sons. Do not go outside, Raffi, and don't open the door to anyone."

"That's going to be hard, I need to go and find Mia."

"Tell her to come here—"

"You don't understand, Pat." Pat noticed Dylan's grey face.

"Dylan? What's happened to you?"

"I gave up drinking, Pat. This morning."

"Why? I mean, that's good—but why?"

"You tell him, Raffi, I think I'm going to be sick."

Pat listened incredulously as Raffi told them of his afternoon, about Dylan and Ollie's dark past and that Dylan was Mia's father.

"Well, that explains a few things doesn't it?" Pat sat down, reeling in the wake of Raffi's story. He recoiled as the door crashed open and Frankie burst in, legs tensed, gun clutched in both hands, ready for action, his eyes darted around the room. He did a double take at the gun Raffi had pointed at his head. Frankie inhaled, straightened and relaxed; he hid his gun behind him.

"Are you okay, Raffi?" he asked.

"Yes and no." Raffi lowered the gun.

"Don't go anywhere, there's a Latino here looking for El Canguro."

"Who's—"

"That's me, Dad. The Kangaroo. That's what they called me in El Rodeo."

"When I catch that fucker, I'm going to hang him on a meat hook in the cold room."

"Frankie! Nic and Patrick are listening." Antoinette pulled her younger son's closer and covered their ears. Nic chortled and Patrick removed his thumb from his mouth and joined in.

"Uncle Frankie's funny," he giggled.

"Mum, take the boys and go to my office. Lock the door and stay there until one of us comes for you. Don't open it until you know it's one of us."

"Come on, do as he says, Antoinette." Pat ushered her and the boys through the clubroom and up to the office.

"Kill the lights as you go, Dad."

Pat flicked off the lights as he left; the loading dock went dark, except for the dim light from the laneway.

****

Dylan groaned and sat down near the dressing room door. Raffi could almost feel his brother's headache.

"What's up, Dylan? Are you sick?" Frankie eyed Dylan's pale face.

"Sober."

"Ah! Raffi's locked you out of the bar, eh?"

"He locked himself out." A twinge of sadness stabbed Raffi as he thought of what Dylan had done for a daughter he didn't know he had less than a week ago.

"What are you doing with that gun, Raffi?"

"Shirley wants me to shoot Dylan."

Frankie's gaze shifted back and forth between Raffi and Dylan.

"Have you been leaving the seat up again, Dylan?"

"No, toast crumbs in the Vegemite." Dylan massaged his temples and moaned. "Tell him, Raffi."

Once again Raffi found himself explaining the events of the week leading to this point where they sat waiting for Shirley's thugs to arrive to collect Ollie's trophies.

"I don't have his fucking trophies, by now the cops have probably got them under a microscope. It wouldn't save him anyway. About the only thing that might save him is my death." Dylan got to his feet, his face the colour of grey chalk. "The one piece of evidence that is really going to hang him he doesn't know about—not yet. Hopefully he won't know it until he's hauled into court."

"What's that?"

"Mia."

"Mia?"

"She's my daughter. Rosie Colter's and mine."

Frankie stared. "She is? But how does that point the finger at Ollie?"

"His DNA and mine were inside Rosie Colter. And his DNA matches that found in the other four victims. If they arrest him, they'll take a swab and he's history."

"Interesting—"

Raffi glanced at his watch. "Well, it's nearly ten p.m."

"I'll just move out of sight—when those arseholes get here, don't look at me, okay?" Frankie flattened himself against the wall.

"What are you going to do?"

"Don't know yet, I'll make it up as I go along." Frankie looked at Dylan. "Have you got something to give Shirley's thugs?"

"Nuh—" Dylan shrugged.

"Would a knuckle sandwich do?" Raffi put in.

"They'll have guns."

"I'll have one, too."

"Raffi, give it to me." Frankie held out his hand.

"No Frankie! You've got kids; you can't afford to go to jail."

"Don't use it, okay."

"I'll try not to."

The hum of an engine and the crunch of tyres reached Raffi's ears; he put his face to the crack in the door to see a white van come to a stop further along the lane.

"We've got company?" Frankie pressed himself against the wall beside the door.

"A van; it's parking along the lane."

Frankie stuck his head around the door. "It's Grennie and his goons. Al and Benji. Grennie always fancied himself as a mobster."

"Grennie? What would Grennie—" Dylan frowned and got to his feet.

"I told you he couldn't be trusted." Raffi's fury boiled.

"Get out of sight, Dylan. You're the one they're gunning for."

"But—"

"Just do as I say, Dylan!" Frankie's face darkened.

Dylan slipped into the darkened doorway that led to the dressing rooms.

"Raffi, get out of sight."

Raffi ducked into the shadow. As Grennie stiff-armed the door, Pat burst through from the clubroom, a roll of gaff tape in his hand.

"Righto! These arseholes—"

Dylan threw himself at Pat as Grennie fired, both men went down. The barrel of Frankie's gun made a sickening thud against Grennie's head and Raffi decked one of his sidekicks with a hard punch to the jaw and poked the muzzle of his gun under the other's ear.

"Drop the gun and lie down!" Raffi's fist sank into his kidney region, the man fell to his knees; the gun slipped from his limp fingers.

Grennie fell beside him, his gun spun across the floor.

"Pat! Dylan! Did he hit you?" Frankie stepped on Grennie's fingers in his haste to gain Pat's side.

"No, but he hit Dylan."

"Dylan!"

Dylan stirred on the floor and moaned. "You alright, Pat?"

"You knocked the wind out of me, but I'm good."

"Dylan, where did he get you."

"In the shoulder." He pushed himself, one-handed, to a sitting position. "Got me through the shoulder. Ho-shit that hurts!"

Benji yelled as Raffi's knee dropped into his back.

"Where are Mia and Kate?"

"Why should I tell you?"

"You better cooperate with us. Shirley is going to jail and so is Ollie. The cops already have the package you're looking for."

"What if I don't cooperate?"

"If you don't I'm going to shoot a hole through your head. Where are they?" Raffi poked his gun behind Benji's ear.

"In the van out the back." He laughed a wheezy laugh. "When Shirley doesn't get what she wants she'll blow it up. This building will blow too."

"What? Is there a bomb in here?"

"Yep. Shirley's only gotta dial the number and pow!"

"Where?"

"Somewhere on the stage but unless you're an expert…"

Frankie stood by listening.

"Dad, take Dylan and get Mum and the boys out of here. You too, Frankie—get out. Frankie!"

Frankie sprinted away through the door to the main clubroom and disappeared.

"Dylan, go and get Antoinette and the boys and take them out the front way."

"You go too, Dad."

"I'm going to tie these bastards up first." He knelt and secured their hands and feet. "Did you dickheads really think you could just walk in here and we'd roll over and piss on our guts?"

Raffi hauled Grennie to his feet and stuck his gun under his ear. "Where's Shirley?"

"Waiting down the lane." Grennie swayed on the spot; he still suffered from the blow to his head.

"You're going to call her off. Tell her—tell her anything, take her fucking phone. Just stop her, or I'll stick a bullet in you. Come on, cunt! Walk!"

"If she sees you holding a gun to my head she'll dial the number—she's nuts mate—"

"Then why the fuck do you do her dirty work?"

"She pays well."

"I pay you well too, arsehole!" Raffi jabbed his fist into Grennie's gut.

"I've got nothing on you. But Shirley? I know so much about her, I could send her down for life—she really pays well."

48

Ollie fretted in the departure lounge of Sydney's International Terminal, his palms as damp as his armpits. His stomach leapt at each boarding announcement and then dropped to the basement when it wasn't his flight. Five times in the last hour he'd had to relieve himself. Oliver Jackson's bladder had never been his strong point. He wore sunglasses and sat isolated from the main crowd, opting for the end of a row, closest to a wall. This behaviour out of character for Ollie, he usually took pains to make himself as visible as possible. His mind wandered, his little brother Dylan had done the unthinkable. He'd turned into such a loser; Ollie always imagined if Dylan did anything he'd take a dive off The Gap. What made him suddenly develop a conscience? Ollie cursed his misplaced confidence in his brother's ongoing silence. He hoped

Shirley's plan had worked and his stepbrother, Raffi, was in custody for Dylan's murder. She believed Raffi's attachment to the girl who sang in his club was sufficient to force his hand. He'd do as instructed and rub out Dylan in an effort to save the girl.

"Dylan is only his stepbrother after all. When push comes to shove, I think Raffi's criminal past will re-emerge."

Ollie didn't share his mother's optimism, so he made his own plan, sweating and fretting in the international departure lounge.

The announcement to board the flight to Moscow joggled Ollie out of his contemplation. He snatched up his hand luggage and entered the jet bridge first. He took his seat and again fretted—he wasn't free yet. He pushed his sunglasses up the bridge of his nose and rubbed his forehead. An eminent senior bureaucrat from the premier's department had just taken the seat across the aisle from him. Ollie cursed himself for buying first class, cattle class would give better anonymity.

"Good evening, Mr Jackson. Off to Europe?"

Ollie nodded and wished he had brought something to read.

****

Mia sat on the floor in the back of the transit van, her hands tied behind her with a cable tie and her ankles tied with another. Kate and an older woman who introduced herself as Miriam Hartwig sat either side of her, tied in the same manner. The man who had imprisoned them into the van took pleasure informing them, if they opened the back door the van would explode. Mia eyed the contraption taped to the back door of the van. She had to assume he told the truth. If she could free herself, they could escape through the side door.

"Keep still, will you?" Miriam snapped at Mia. All three women had managed to nudge the gags from their mouths.

"I'm trying to free myself." Mia wriggled her bottom between her arms, puffing and struggling she manoeuvred her hands in front of her. She used her teeth to tighten the thin cable tie on her wrists.

"You're tightening it, silly girl." The older woman raised an imperious eyebrow at Mia and she resisted telling her to fuck off. She rose to her knees and wedged her elbows hard past her hipbones.

"Silly girl, you can't break—"

The zip tie fell away.

"Little trick I learned from the internet. Can I borrow your necklace?"

"My necklace?"

Mia didn't wait for permission, she removed Miriam's thin silver snake chain necklace and used it to saw through the zip tie on her ankles.

"Good thinking," said Kate.

Mia severed the ties on Miriam and Kate's ankles and opened the side door on the van.

"Quickly!"

"Aren't you going to untie our hands?" The woman's haughty manner irritated Mia.

"Don't you want to get away from that bomb?"

"Of course I do."

"Then shut up and climb out."

"Come on," said Kate, "hurry up before someone sees us."

Mia had used this lane many times over the past months, at this hour on a Monday night it stood deserted. She led them to a walkway, down the concrete stairs of an underground car park.

****

Shirley's impatience got the better of her and she moved into the end of the darkened lane. She waited for Grennie to bring Ollie's trophy box and her old diaries. If she didn't get them, she'd blow the whole lot--Pat, his whore, and their bastards. Pat had predictably gathered his mistress and their children under the one roof. Dylan and his lowlife wife, Kate. Miriam—Ollie's mother-in-law—that bitch always thought herself superior to Shirley. Tonight, all their lives depended on Shirley getting what she wanted.

Grennie stumbled from the back door of Raffi's House of Blues and teetered towards her. He appeared dazed as he shrugged his shoulders. His upturned palms meant he had failed to retrieve what Dylan had stolen. Grennie drew level with the van.

"To hell with you too, Grennie. You know way too much." She poked her phone to life and sent the text messages to the phones Touchy Trevor had bodgied. The ERM motor would buzz and set off the bombs. The shockwave ruffled her hair and tugged at her cheeks, the van expelled outward as it burst into flames. Ears ringing, Shirley trotted to the end of the lane as fast as her sixty-seven year old legs would carry her. As she emerged at the edge of the busy street, she stopped. Why hadn't the nightclub exploded? Touchy Trevor said that bomb was powerful enough to kill everyone in the building. A siren sounded somewhere in the distance, Shirley backed away in a panic, stumbled and screamed as a speeding taxi broke her fall, she rattled across the bonnet and hit the windscreen. Her head smashed a dent in the laminated glass.

49

Raffi aimed the gun at Grennie's back and sighted the white transit van parked along the lane; he hurried down the steps—if he could get there before Shirley blew it… An explosion punched the air and knocked him on his back and a scream filled his ears, his heart broke at a love blown apart. Ears buzzing, he rose to his knees, clutched the gun, and searched for an enemy target. The achromatic streetlight at the lane entrance lit the edges of the acrid smoke billowing from the van. Great rags of flame curled around the wreckage, scorching the air. Grennie had vanished in the smoke. A screech of tyres and shouts rang out from the end of the lane. Somewhere in the back of his mind, he knew Frankie had succeeded in disarming the bomb inside the club.

Raffi got to his feet and a cold, hard object jabbed the back of his neck.

"Kneel, El Canguro, and drop the gun."

****

"Quickly! Down here, don't fall." Mia put her arm around Miriam's shoulders. As they reached the first landing, a blast shook the building; the van had exploded in the lane. A draft of air whooshed down the stairwell and tugged at their clothing and hair. Mia held on to Miriam to prevent her fall. Kate clutched the handrail and whimpered at the orange glow above them.

****

The slippery accent, Raffi recognised from two and a half years in South America. The adrenaline that pulsed after the explosion slowed, and he grew calm as he sank to his knees. He didn't care if he died now. Mia was dead, why should he live on? Time slowed as he waited for the bullet to tear through his spine. A thud and a grunt came from behind; the gun barrel scraped his skin as a hurtling body knocked him to his hands and knees.

"Okay scum, let the gun go and get to your feet." Frankie's words flowed silky-calm. "No sudden moves or I'll blow the top off your head."

Raffi scrambled to his feet, picked up his gun and noticed the surprised Colombian's neck had Frankie's sinewy arm clamped around it. Frankie had his gun poked in the man's ear.

"You don't know who you're messing with!"

"I think I do. You're Santiago Mazo."

"I am *El Gato.*"

"I'm a Frenchman—in my language Gateau is a cake."

"El Gato!"

"Oh yes, gato. You're a pussy? Well, let me tell you what they called me when I was in Brazil. They called me *El Cirujeno.*"

"Let's get him inside, Frankie." The wail of sirens approached.

"Come, Santiago. I must prep you for surgery."

Raffi locked the back door of the club, stepped over Benji and Al and followed Frankie as he jogged Santiago through the clubroom, up the stairs to the foyer and into the lift. With his gun still stuck under the Colombian's ear, he pressed the lift button with his elbow. Upstairs, he marched him into the restaurant kitchen.

"Keep him covered, Raffi."

Raffi aimed his gun at Santiago's face and watched as his uncle went to work on the Colombian gangster, gagging him with a generous wrapping of gaff tape. Raffi's mind clung to Mia. The only girl he had ever loved. She was dead.

Why am I still here—alive?

Frankie frisked the Colombian and removed a knife from his jacket. He shoved Santiago in front of him, the gun against his backbone.

"Open the cold-room, Raffi."

Raffi did as instructed, pulled the cold-room open and Frankie forced the man inside. Raffi pulled the door closed behind them and watched as Frankie secured the man's wrists together with more wraps of the gaff tape, raised the hitman's hands above his head, and secured them to a meat hook. Raffi was thankful his uncle didn't hurt him—he even left his feet on the floor.

"Tape his ankles together, Raffi."

Raffi wrapped Santiago's ankles with gaff tape.

"Okay, come on; let's hide these guns before the police arrive."

He closed the cold-room and snapped the lock. He took Raffi's gun and burrowed it with his own and Santiago's under several trays of frozen oysters in the deep freeze.

"Quickly, downstairs."

They raced back to the loading dock, past Shirley's thugs, still trussed up on the floor and opened the back door. A police car pulled up in the lane way followed by a fire truck. Red and blue lights pulsed in time with Raffi's heart.

"What happened to the bomb on the stage?"

"I diffused it. Pretty easy—all I had to do was take the battery out of the phone they had rigged as a trigger. Amateurs."

Raffi leaned on the wall and covered his face the tears he'd been fighting flowed.

"I'm sorry, Raffi. When I get my hands on old Shirley, she is going to pay; I don't care if I have to go to jail."

"I'll help you."

"The hell you will. If I go to jail, it will be well past time. I've done a lot of bad shit and jail is probably where I belong, but know this, Raff, I've never harmed anyone who didn't have it coming."

"What are you going to do with the guy in the cold room?"

"He's next week's pork roast."

50

Mia led Kate and Miriam across the car park and stopped at the bottom of the stairs. She used the necklace to cut the zip ties still binding their wrists.

"We need to find a phone box," said Kate.

Grennie had taken her bag and with it, Mia's phone and wallet.

"Phone boxes are a thing of the past." Miriam marched into a Seven-Eleven and told the young man behind the counter she must use his phone. Mia made a note; she had to learn to be so imperious; the young man handed his mobile over without hesitation. After Miriam made her call, she handed the phone to Kate who tried to call Dylan. His phone went to voice mail. She left a quick message and then called Raffi. He answered after one ring.

"Raffi—whoa! Calm down—she's with me. We're in the mall—You are? Okay we'll be right there."

Mia scooted out the door as Kate passed the phone back to the Seven-Eleven cashier and thanked him.

The sight of an ambulance in front of Raffi's House of Blues scared both Mia and Kate. Raffi met them on the step and scooped Mia into a hard embrace.

"Mia!" He squeezed the air out of her lungs. He kissed her forehead, her cheeks and lips. "I thought you were dead—Mia—"

"We got out just in time—" Mia clung to him.

"Dylan!"

Mia twisted around at the frightened cry behind her. Paramedics wheeled Dylan on a stretcher, they stopped while Kate hugged and kissed her husband. Mia didn't know why, but she trembled at the sight of Dylan on the stretcher with a bloody dressing across his shoulder and a drip in his arm. Her feet carried her to his side.

"Mia—I'm so glad you're safe." He forced a smiled onto his bloodless face.

"What happened?" Mia couldn't control her trembling lips and the tears rolling down her face.

"I did what I do best, sweetheart. I got in the way."
He gave her hand a brief squeeze. "Are you all right?"

"I'm fine."

"Thank god."

She swallowed and tried to hold back the tears as she watched the paramedics wheel him away, Kate held his hand as she walked beside the trolley. Raffi's arm slipped around Mia's waist.

"I—Raffi, is he badly hurt?" She whispered.

"He was shot in the shoulder, one of Shirley's men tried to shoot Dad and Dylan jumped in front of him."

Mia couldn't contend with the ache in her chest. Why did it upset her so? He was her mother's rapist.

"It's okay to be upset, Mia. Whatever else he is, he is your father. He's your closest living relative. He's not a bad man—he made a hideous mistake when he was a kid—he spent this morning talking to a solicitor, trying to make amends for what he did. I don't think anyone could have known what old Shirley would do."

51

As he'd done at least once a minute since boarding, Oliver Jackson checked his watch; the plane should have taken off ten minutes before. The stewards had closed the doors; he quaked inside at what might be the hold up. One engine started, then another, and he imagined he heard the next whine into action. Ollie inhaled and blew it out slowly; he wiped his palms on his thighs.

Why aren't we moving? Just leave already!

One by one, the engines powered down and the captain's voice sounded through the PA.

"Good evening ladies and gentlemen, we will be experiencing a brief delay. Please remain in your seats as we attend to the matter. We appreciate your patience and apologise for the inconvenience."

Ollie's heart thudded heavily and dread scorched his body from the inside. He rose; he'd just lock himself in the restroom.

****

10.30 p.m., Will Fishman and his assistant waited at the Mascot Police Station. With Lloyd Beaufort's tipoff that Oliver Jackson prepared to flee the country, Will had had to hand the task of arresting him to the Federal Police; he had no jurisdiction in the airport. It left a bitter taste in Will's mouth, he'd longed for the day when he might get the chance to arrest the Sand Dune Killer. The dream had faded to regret as the years passed.

The Commissioner had predictably slowed Will down.

"Oliver Jackson is a decent man and a long serving member of the legislative assembly."

"I'm sorry, sir, but I have conclusive evidence. He is the Sand Dune Killer. No doubt about it."

"I've been friends with Oliver for years, this can't be true!"

"His brother has come forward—handed himself in—"

"His brother! That alcoholic, womanising rogue!"

"You can't stand in the way of justice—"

"Fine! Arrest him," the commissioner waggled a finger at Will, *"but if I'm proved right, I'll have your badge!"*

"If I'm proved wrong, sir, I'll give you my badge on a silver platter, along with a whip to flog my miserable arse."

Will drummed his fingers on the arm of the chair and tapped his foot; he wanted this over. Not because he wanted to get home to bed—he didn't think he'd sleep for a week after the events of this day. He wanted to see The Sand Dune Killer behind bars. He wanted to see him punished for the lives he'd taken. Punished for the lives he had destroyed.

"Can I get you another coffee, Will?"

"No thank you, Steph—Christ! How long does it take to pull that butt-crumb off a plane?"

****

The steward pushed the door open the door and spoke briefly to someone out of Ollie's line of vision. His heart dropped into his boots as he caught sight of the unmistakable uniform of a federal police officer; the steward pointed in Ollie's direction. A ringing in Ollie's ears blocked the whispers around him; he had a sense of floating above himself, isolated in a sensory deprivation chamber. The officers took an age to reach him, then he found himself gazing at the familiar kangaroo and emu emblem with the words 'Police' under them—the badge of a federal police officer. His words—something about being under arrest and accompanying them to the Mascot police station barely registered. His head spun and his face burned as the officers handcuffed and cautioned him. Oliver Jackson's humiliation was absolute when his eyes met those of the astounded bureaucrat who sat opposite. As the police led him towards the door, rows of faces stared and whispered—Ollie's hopes of anonymity proved futile given he'd spent the past eighteen years ensuring everyone in Sydney knew him. Oliver Jackson; widely touted as a future premier of New South Wales—even future prime minister.

Back through the jet bridge they led him—his ultimate walk of shame—through the airport to a waiting car. The hand on his head pushed him into the back seat, the final crumb of his dishonour.

****

The sweet faced WPC put her head around the door and said the words Will had waited twenty years to hear.

"Your prisoner is now in state custody, Superintendent; he is waiting for you in the interview room."

Will sprung to his feet; he had to resist punching the air and he restrained himself from kissing the young woman.

"This way, please, Superintendent Fishman."

Will tried hard to keep the spring from his stride as he followed the constable through the door and along the corridor to the interview room.

"I'll have your badge for this, Fishman!" Oliver Jackson sneered, "You and all your bungling, incompetent officers."

"Relax, Jackson, we'll get you processed and over to headquarters by about midnight I should imagine."

"When my attorney gets here you will release me."

"Don't bet on it, mate. The assault and rape of your wife has been added to the rape and murder charges."

"Don't be ridiculous!"

"She made a statement to us about three hours ago. You beat her up pretty badly, made you feel good did it? Just like old times?"

Will enjoyed watching Oliver Jackson's sweaty face take on a deathly pallor; his head swivelled this way and that, from Will to the Police Custody Officer, to the door and back. He reminded Will of a cornered meerkat. A knock on the door told Will the sweet faced WPC returned.

"Superintendent, can I have a word?"

Will stepped outside and closed the door.

"Oliver's mother was struck by a car about an hour ago. She's dead. Her husband, Pat Rooney has informed us she is responsible for the van explosion in a lane way in King's Cross. One of her cohorts died. The other two have been taken into custody and they've both given statements against Shirley. It sounds as if she ordered the kidnap of three women, including Oliver's mother-in-law and sister-in-law. They held them hostage in the van. The women managed to escape just before the explosion. The forensic unit is down there now, they have her mobile. She also planted a bomb in the Raffi's House of Blues Nightclub Complex but the chef diffused it—"

"The chef?"

"He's a bit of a dark horse by the sounds of it, not many chefs know how to diffuse a bomb."

"Normally I'd be deeply suspicious but in this case I'll look the other way. Well, I guess I'd better give Mr Jackson the bad news. Thanks, Constable Nilsson. Is that car ready to take him down to headquarters?"

"Yes, sir, whenever you're ready. Oh, and sir?"

"Yes?"

"There's a group of journalists out the front—they've heard the feds arrested Oliver Jackson and they want a story."

"What have you told them so far?"

"Nobody has made any comment."

"Got to tread carefully, Constable, I don't want to upset the powers that be. I'll talk to them—lead the way."

He left the PCO to monitor the door that detained Oliver Jackson. The reception area swelled with reporters and camera crews.

Why do they bother? They know I'm not going to tell them anything.

"Superintendent Fishman, why has Oliver Jackson been arrested?"

"Why is a senior officer of the New South Wales Police attending…?"

"Can you tell us…?"

Will waved the reporters quiet and cleared his throat.

"Good evening. Tonight at ten forty-eight pm at Sydney Airport, a federal police team arrested a senior public figure in connection with a historical offence. The person is now in New South Wales police custody and is assisting us with our inquiries. We'll give a press release as soon as it is appropriate. Thank you ladies and gentlemen and goodnight."

Will turned on his heel and left the room as quickly as he entered; the snapping of cameras and the journalists' questions faded as the door closed behind him.

52

Four a.m. and the forensics still toiled. Chequered police tape cordoned off Raffi's House of Blues main clubroom and loading dock. They told Raffi he could use the office, as long as no one came through the cordon. They collected the Parcel Post box and the bubble wrap. They also took the hard drives from the security system but given Raffi had switched the system off after the parcel delivery, he didn't think they would be of much use. He and Frankie stood alone in the foyer, Pat had gone home and Mia was asleep on the couch in Raffi's office.

"What are you going to do with old mate up there in the cold-room?"

"I told you, he's next week's pork roast."

"Bullshit—we can't just keep him in there indefinitely."

"I'm going to re-educate him and send him home to Colombia."

"Do you want my help?"

"Where is Mia?"

"She is curled up asleep on the couch in my office. That poor bastard up there must be nearly frozen to death by now."

"Nah—he's okay. I turned the fan off."

"So, how do you go about re-educating him?"

"I'll need your laptop, mine is at home, and bring the key for the lift. Might be prudent to lock it off while we enlighten our prisoner."

Raffi didn't ask why his uncle needed his laptop but he went to fetch it. Before he left his office, he paused, the belief he'd lost Mia had elicited a pain deep inside. Then she turned up safe and sound, but like a physical injury, the ache persisted. He smiled as he watched her, curled on the couch, her dark hair spilled across her face crumpled into the cushion, her full lips cherubic—relaxed in a deep sleep. His loins stirred a little as he observed the gentle rise and fall of her chest, her breasts squashed between her arms. The curve of her hip tempted him to curl up against her.

He dragged his eyes away and clicked the door behind him as he left.

On the top floor, Raffi used his key to disable the lift. Frankie set the laptop on a table in the restaurant, switched it on and did a quick Google search.

"All right," he said, "bring it into the cold-room."

Frankie slid the door of the cold-room and left it open, Raffi couldn't help but feel sorry for Santiago, standing shivering with his hands trussed above his head.

"So, El Gato—it's a bit cold—no? Makes the old pizzle shrivel, doesn't it?" Frankie raised a butcher's knife and held it poised, in the manner of an artist with a loaded brush, contemplating his canvas. He tilted his head, "Ah, but where to begin—"

Raffi joined the game.

"How about at the brisket? Brisket to balls is always good." He trusted Frankie kidded, the black eyes glittered dangerously but Raffi knew his uncle had a great poker face.

"Please—I do my job, this is all—you know how it is?"

"No, I don't actually. I've never worked for a scummy bastard who would order me to kill an innocent man."

"But El Canguro—he kill Felipé Carrel—"

"The hell I did! That little fucker was alive and well when I left Bogota. I was proved innocent."

"*Mi jefe*—my boss—he's very sad to lose his son."

"Killing the wrong man isn't going to bring him back."

"Ah—you explain that to Manuel."

"Manuel is dead."

Santiago opened his mouth to speak but as Frankie's words sank in, he shut it again. Raffi glanced at Frankie, was he bluffing?

"No, no—" Santiago began.

"When did you leave Colombia, Santiago?"

"Five days ago."

"I left there two days ago, Manuel is finished."

"No, *tú mientes!* Y—You lie!"

"No, I tell the truth. Raffi, roll that news footage on the computer?"

He touched the screen and held it for Santiago to watch, Raffi tried to follow the Spanish language news report but missed most of it. The Colombian blinked, the computer screen reflected in his eyes as he watched and shook his head, in spite of the cold air, beads of sweat oozed from his face.

"So you see, Santiago—this is why I didn't kill you. I'm giving you a chance to turn your life around, sneak home and keep your head down. Stay out of trouble."

Santiago stared, his swarthy complexion turned sallow. He flinched as Frankie brandished the knife before him and sliced through the entwining gaff tape that held him to the butcher's hook.

"You are free to leave, Santiago, but before you go."

Santiago's face, one moment relieved, turned fearful.

"S—Sí?"

"Can I offer you some breakfast?"

53

Within the pale walls of the holding cell, Ollie reflected on his life. At five years old he'd learned the thrill of hurting things when he squeezed a kitten, it yowled and attacked him. Ollie's hatred of cats set in stone as he bawled to his unsympathetic maternal grandmother about the scratches and teeth marks on his hands. His grandmother loved cats and hated Ollie. She told him Owen Delaney wasn't his father.

"That's why you're not as handsome as he is."

When Ollie asked his mother for the truth, she confirmed it. Owen Delaney had been distant though never unkind, and the only father Ollie had known. His grandmother died soon after and Ollie fantasised he had killed her with his bare hands. Ollie both loved and hated his mother, he wanted to punish her but she was his mother. Ollie grew to hate women.

At seven, he dropped a knee onto the back of a friend's guinea pig and pretended it was an accident. A strange but pleasant sensation flooded his loins as it twitched, he hadn't intended to kill it—just maim, but he smiled his secret smile as the urine leaked from the convulsing rodent and it took its last breath. Poetry. He'd often castigated himself on taking so long to find his heart. At nine years old he made his first premeditated kill. A kitten in the park, helpless, furry little thing with big blue eyes. It screeched when he stomped on it and Ollie enjoyed watching the life slowly leave the tiny twitching body after he bludgeoned its head with a rock. Over the years, he tried different ways of killing—a rock to the head remained his preferred method. As big a rock as he could lift—smaller rocks didn't have the immediate and decisive impact that made his heart sing. Taking a life was akin to divine power and Ollie wanted divinity. The first girl he raped pleaded with him not to kill her, he beat her up and told her if she reported it, he'd find her and kill her. It worked; the girl kept her silence but it left him empty—incomplete. Two years later, the ever-present urge to kill possessed him. The need to dominate—rape—terrorise then end it with a rock overwhelmed. He adopted his secret name, Blitz. The media called him The Sand Dune Killer. Did they realise the inspiration he gained by the title they gave? His last kill was the girl at Bundeena, Blitz had sailed much too close to the wind that time and had had to control his urge to kill. Shirley made him remove the tattoo and promise no more killing.

Finally, Pat had spoiled it for Ollie. Peppi Ender's daughter Marie, whined to her father that Ollie took her hard up the arse, bit her all over the shoulders and almost strangled her. Peppi sent Col McInnis to whack him.

Peppi, the passionate Italian father. Talk about over reaction! Marie should have been grateful I let her live.

Pat and that insignificant French chef saved him, Ollie had once again escaped punishment, but Pat; the old bastard twigged, he knew Ollie was up to something and he kept a gimlet eye on him. So much so, Ollie asked himself if there existed a way to have power without killing. He could be a king but the nearest Australia had to a king was the Prime Minister. Ollie would be Prime Minister.

"Mum, how do you get into politics?"

"Join a union I think," said Shirley.

Ollie had asked Pat—like him or not, Pat was smarter than Shirley.

"The easiest way, Ol, is go to university and study political science."

"University?" A smarmy smile had contorted Ollie's twisted features; he could easily imagine himself wearing a mortarboard and gown. That in itself would give him prestige and power.

He found it a struggle, but four years after he began, Ollie graduated a fully-fledged politician. All he lacked was a seat in parliament. He had joined the party during university and volunteered at every opportunity. Ollie never missed a chance to bring himself to the attention of the hierarchy. He'd had to nominate for preselection three times before his chance arose. In a bi-election in a marginal seat, he had scraped in but then lost it at the following general election. He'd spent another four years in limbo, once again performing at an administrative level. His big break came when the party parachuted him into a safe seat and he won. Oliver Jackson served in a government that just fell over the line. Ollie secured a portfolio and his career forged ahead. Being Pat Rooney's stepson held an advantage. Well-known identity in Sydney society—Pat's name carried a certain amount of power. Former NRL star—well known publican and nightclub owner. The fact he had knocked up his sixteen-year-old employee hadn't hurt his reputation one bit in Ollie's opinion.

Now that perfect life crumbled around him. Oliver's only ally was dead. He told Shirley to stay out of it, that he'd simply slip out of the country, but no—his mother had fancied herself as an underworld kingpin. She exploded a hire company's empty van and then stepped in front of a speeding Silver Top.

Stupid woman.

His darling wife showed her true colours—the rape and assault charges his attorney thought he might evade— he would plead temporary insanity, the stress of discovering his wife's affair with his brother drove him to it. Ollie had refused to give a DNA sample but Heather (treacherous cow) had allowed them to take a DNA sample from her and it matched that of the Sand Dune Killer.

Ollie's lower lip trembled as he sat alone, he tried to remember his secret smile but his mouth refused. The world had turned on him, his political colleagues had fallen over one another as they scrambled to distance themselves from Oliver Jackson—Blitz—The Sand Dune Killer.

54

Mia's stomach fluttered, this would be the first time she acknowledged Dylan Delaney as her father. Raffi had offered to accompany her and it tempted her to have him along, but she knew this had to be between her and Dylan.

"Take the lift to level seven and turn left along the corridor," a woman behind the hospital reception desk pointed. "Mr Delaney is in room nine."

"Thanks." Mia abandoned her attempt at a smile, squared her shoulders, and marched to the lift.

She stopped before door number nine, inhaled and knocked.

"Come in."

Her hand shook as she pushed the door and entered. "Hello."

"Mia." Dylan smiled then grimaced as he used the trapeze bar to haul himself up on the pillows. "I'm glad you're here."

Mia's eyes welled as she sat on the chair beside his bed.

"I don't know what words to use to tell you how sorry I am for what I did to your mother."

She shook her head, the words she had planned for that moment evaporated.

"But here I am, looking at my daughter, one I don't deserve—one that shouldn't be, but I'm happy she is."

Mia smiled and the flood of tears she could hold no longer fell. She sobbed into her hands.

"I'm sorry for how I treated you. I had no excuse, I—" Dylan's voice faltered.

"You weren't to know. I shouldn't—"

"No, you did nothing wrong, it was me who was wrong."

There wasn't a thing either could do to change the past, Mia wanted to forget it happened. After all, she had a life and she wanted it to be happy, not full of recrimination and regret.

"What can I do, Mia? To make it right?"

"There's nothing—you've already made it right by confessing—" His hand closed around her wrist and their eyes met.

"It was Ollie who hit her with the rock. I wish I could have stopped him, I've gone over it a million times and I didn't know he would do what he did."

"I'm going to hear it in court—I'm determined I'm going to sit every day and look at the man who destroyed my family."

"I'll sit with you, Mia. If I'm able—I won't let you down."

"It means a lot to find I still have family."

"I'm probably not the kind of family you had wished for, but I'm here and I promise you, I'll be the best father a girl could hope for. Please believe me." He drew her to him and Mia rose and allowed him to pull him against him in a one-armed embrace.

"Dylan?" Kate's arrival broke them apart. Mia sat back on the chair and wiped her eyes.

"Kate," Dylan's voice sounded thick with tears he still to shed. "Come here. I have something to tell you."

Kate blenched.

"Hey, stop worrying—I love you pretty lady and—judge willing—I'll be the best husband and father you and our baby could hope for."

Kate brushed past Mia as she hastened to him, her arms closed around his neck.

"Careful, girl. My shoulder is pretty sore."

Mia watched her father kiss his wife; she worried she intruded.

"Kate, sit down. You'll need to be seated for what I'm about to tell you."

Is Kate going to like me?

Mia feared the older woman's reaction—she hadn't been friendly in the past, would this make things worse?

"You know how I worried if I'd make a good dad?"

"You'll be fine if you put your mind to it." Kate patted his good arm.

"I'm already a dad."

"What?"

"Mia is my daughter—I only found out last week."

"But how—"

Mia stared at the floor as Dylan told Kate of the daughter he never knew he had.

"…so there you have it, Kate. Proves that something so wrong can turn out right. It's still wrong, I know. I can't change what happened back then. There's nothing else I can do but make the best of it."

Kate's eyes moved from her husband to his daughter. Mia could think of nothing to say, she couldn't change the past; her birth a pure accident. She speculated why her grandparents didn't have her aborted, her grandfather Kerrod Colter was a Catholic and she supposed the reason. An ethics committee must have sanctioned her birth—it would have taken more than her grandparent's wishes. She couldn't imagine the bravery required for her grandmother to accept the fruit of the violence that took her daughter's life. Until she read Lily's diaries, she assumed herself the product of a teenage pregnancy that went badly wrong. Not a word of resentment had escaped her grandmother's mouth, as a child, she had known only cherishment.

"I don't know what to say. I need time—"

Mia nodded. "I understand."

"We've plenty of time—in fact we have all the time in the world."

The three of them started. Raffi and Pat burst in the door.

"Actually, you only have a couple of months, Dylan."

Dylan's face turned pale. "For what?"

"To practice your moves," said Raffi. "Work on Dylan's Cocktail Lounge will start next week and I'll expect you on deck to manage it when it opens."

55

Mia sat between Kate and Dylan, watched the jury file into the courtroom and take their seats.

"People of the jury, have you reached a verdict?"

The foreman of the jury got to his feet; he had grey hair and a hawkish face. "We have your honour."

The bailiff took a note from the foreman and passed it up to the judge. Mia glanced up at Dylan and followed his gaze, his brother sat with his head bowed and shoulders drooping.

"On the count of first degree murder of Tahnee Shultz, how do you find?"

"Guilty, Your Honour."

"On the count of aggravated sexual assault of Tahnee Shultz, how do you find?"

"Guilty, Your Honour."

"On the count of first degree murder of Zoe Johnson, how do you find?"

"Guilty, Your Honour."

"On the count of…"

Mia imitated Dylan and kept her eyes on Oliver Jackson. She pitied him, sitting motionless, arms hanging straight, hands loosely clasped between his thighs. He made no sign he even listened as the judge recited his crimes and asked for the verdict.

"On the count of voluntary manslaughter of Rosalie Colter, how do you find?"

"Guilty, Your Honour." Mia's eye flicked from Jackson to the jury foreman, their eyes met and lingered. The foreman turned back to the judge.

Mia sighed and wished her grandparents could have lived long enough to hear his words. The judge banged his gavel and the words "All rise" made her realise she had zoned out for the final verdict.

Raffi greeted her as she left the court with Kate and Dylan. He, his parents and Frankie didn't attend many of the court sittings over the past eight months. Mia had attended all. Dylan missed a few when Kate gave birth to his second daughter.

Scott Matthews and Lloyd joined them on the pavement.

"Are you okay, Dylan?" Scott gently pushed a reporter aside. "Please, give my client his privacy."

"Yeah, I'm good. So what happens now?"

"Ollie will be sentenced late next week and then I guess his team will launch an appeal. This will probably drag on for years."

"What do you think he'll get?"

"Life. And if Justice Marsden is as brave as I think he is, he'll tack on a never to be released clause."

56

Raffi sat beside Mia, his arm around her shoulders; the familiar jolt kicked him somewhere below the navel as she smiled up at him. This time next week, they would be in Paris but tonight, Raffi happily anticipated the event he'd longed for since old enough to appreciate his parent's situation. They dressed Rose d'Orléans Café up for the wedding of the decade. He and Frankie had laboured all day to make it perfect. Raffi smiled as he watched his father, waiting for his bride. Twenty-six years after the birth of their first son, Pat would finally make Antoinette his wife. He, Frankie and Dylan had had a back yard bonfire and Shirley's diaries went up in a cloud of acrid smoke. Raffi wasn't privy to the contents of those diaries and best he didn't know.

He smiled as his parents made their vows, those they had lived by since the day they met. Hours later, the bride and groom prepared to farewell their family and friends. Antoinette turned her back and tossed the bouquet too high, too hard. It bounced off the ceiling, glanced off her brother's head and landed in Raffi's lap.

THE END

JACOL PUBLISHING

www.JaColpublishing.com invites you to peruse all our books.

A. Isobel also has *Georgie Angel*, as well as two fantasy novels. Please join our family of authors in celebrating the work we have endeavored to bring to the public.

Bio

A. Isobel Sutcliffe lives in Western Queensland, Australia with her husband, two dogs and two cats. She has an adult son and daughter. A child of grazier parents in rural Queensland she spent thirty-three years working as a musician, playing in pubs and nightclubs. A visual artist she turned to writing in 2015. This is her second romance/suspense.

JACOL PUBLISHING

www.JaColpublishing.com invites you to peruse all our books.

A. Isobel also has *Georgie Angel*, as well as two fantasy novels. Please join our family of authors in celebrating the work we have endeavored to bring to the public.